DRY HEAT

A NOVEL

Steven Eggleton

ISBN: 0615624340
ISBN-13: 978-0615624341

This book is dedicated
to the Big Six…
go fuck yourself.

Special thanks to all those who
helped
in editing my work.

ACKNOWLEDGMENTS

Acknowledgment is made to the editors of *Struggle: A Magazine of Proletarian Revolutionary Literature*, *Mobius: The Journal of Social Change*, and *The Iconoclast* where some of these chapters originally appeared.

CHAPTER 1
(September)

I hated my job. Everyday I left smelling like roast beef and fried chicken. My pants had permanent grease stains on them, and bits of smooshed cheese permanently resided in the tracks of the musty old shoes I wore to work. Where were the riches, pussy and fame MTV had promised me? Had it all been a lie?

I don't know why, but growing up I always thought things would just happen for me. I guess I figured I was special. I mean, can you blame me? My generation had spent more time watching TV than any generation before us. Our brains had been rotted by MTV and Nick at Night.

I had grown up thinking I'd graduate high school, land the perfect job, marry a super model, and live happily ever after. The people on TV always had everything they wanted. I thought the same would happen for me. It looked so effortless. I figured this was America and everyone would get their slice of the pie while canned laughter played in the background. What a crock! I had been brainwashed a half-hour at a time all my life. I never imagined I'd be so, ordinary.

At any rate, work was a funny thing. I couldn't think of any other institution, that required one to spend 8 hours a day in a cramped space, with people you couldn't stand. My personal slice of hell was a grocery store deli with a bunch of women in their late 30's and early 40's.

This pack of hens constantly bickered, complained, menstruated, and formed and broke alliances. They bitched about their husbands and boyfriends. Sometimes they treated me like a kid brother, and other times like they wanted to fuck me. The manager, Brenda, was fat and doughy and lazy as all hell. She stared at the world through dirty glasses and suffered from chronic gas. She liked to flirt with the delivery men and wear loud makeup. One day, hung-over as all hell, I let her blow me in the back cooler (not one of my finer moments), while I leaned back against a pallet of Swiss cheese. It didn't mean anything, it was just one of those fucked up things that occasionally happen, when you're horny and forced to work with someone in close quarters for days on end. After it happened, we never talked about the incident, and we pretended like it hadn't occurred. It was better that way.

The store was about a mile from the university so a number of our customers were spoiled little rich kids going to school, out of state, on mommy and daddy's dime (not unlike my girlfriend).

I hated waiting on people my own age, actually I hated waiting on all people, but especially university students. I never understood the fervor with which most Tucsonans supported the University. They'd cover themselves and their cars with all kinds of crappy red and blue collegiate propaganda, and foam at the mouth in anticipation of the next sporting event. The funny thing was, most of them had never even seen the inside of a classroom. They couldn't tell a university from a unicycle. I guess people just need to feel like they're a part of something. To belong. Myself included.

The college kids were a constant reminder of what a fuck-up I was. I had done a few semesters at community college, but when it started to interfere with my social life I had to give it up. Besides, I didn't even have a major. I had mostly gone to appease my parents. It was all bullshit posturing. Nothing interested me. I was aimless. I wanted to coast through life and be left alone. I wasn't interested in being a master of industry. If it didn't have long legs and a skirt, count me out.

One night, around closing, a skinny little sorority girl, with perfect teeth and pointy little upturned elf-boobs, started ringing the counter-bell like her shirt was on fire. I was in back washing dishes –alone. I finished rinsing the pan in my hand then sauntered out to the front counter as slow as humanly possible. This was my typical, passive-aggressive, move when someone pounded on the bell like an asshole. I had to be careful these days, though, I was on probation for telling too many customers to get bent, one more time and I would be out the door, and as much as I hated this job, I still desperately needed it.

As I came around the corner elf-boobs looked at me in disgust. I was sweaty, covered in grease, and needed a shave. She on the other hand, looked as pristine as the Virgin Mary. I could see the outline of her erect nipples under the thin fabric of her Clash t-shirt. She wasn't wearing any bra, but she didn't have a need for one either. She was young, taut and perky. I could feel contempt and lust for her boiling inside of me. Hell, she probably didn't even know who Mick Jones was.

"Are you open?" she sneered.

"Not when you ring the bell like that," I countered under my breath.

"What did you say?"

"Nothing. How can I help you," I forced out.

"Give me a pound of coleslaw," she snarled.

I surmised she must have a sick rabbit back in her dorm room. There was no way this skinny bitch was gonna eat a pound of coleslaw. But I decided to give her "the old special treatment" just in case it was for her.

"Sure," I said suddenly finding myself in a better mood. " One second. I already put it in the back."

At night we had to pull all the salads out of the case, wrap them in cling film, and store them in the back cooler. Otherwise the stores fluorescent lights would zap them of all their color and make them look sickly.

I walked around the corner smiling to myself. Eager to exact my revenge. I grabbed a one pound container, entered the cooler and filled it half way up with slaw. Then, from deep inside my soul, I hocked up a thick, meaty, green loogie (it even had a nostril hair in it) and spit it into the middle of her cabbage salad. Then I packed more slaw on top of it and walked back around the corner.

"Here ya go." I said merrily. "Anything else for ya?"

"No. Thank you," she sassed.

As I watched the bitch's narrow ass disappear into the distance I was filled with self loathing. What was I doing with my life? There wasn't any reason I couldn't be attending the university. I was smart. Was this to be my destiny? Working a soul crushing job, day after day, like my father?

After the army, he had spent his life being bamboozled by the gas company. First as a meter-reading grunt in the field, then as a low level supervisor in an office cubicle. He had sold his soul for a slice of the American pie and instead received an ulcer and a quaint little house in a working class neighborhood. It was a sham. All his hard work had amounted to a hill of beans. As the corporations grew stronger the working class grew weaker. They gave you enough to survive, barely. But the rest of the time they dangled the carrot out of your reach. It was the world's greatest con. I finished cleaning up the deli, turned off all the lights, punched out, and made my way up front.

Chapter 2
(September)

I wasn't even sure I wanted to go, I had to work the next day, but a bunch of the gang were going down to the Loft theater for a ten o'clock showing of *A Clockwork Orange*. I had never seen it and didn't understand what the big deal was. I was 22. It was 1999.

"It's Stanley Kubrick. You'll love it," Roo (a knick-name appropriated from her favorite Winnie-the-Pooh character) assured me.

I figured, what the heck, why not go. I walked back to Roo's room and pulled out my pipe. It had come to the point where I couldn't do anything without getting high first. It just made everything better. Whether it was going out to eat, watching a movie, fucking, or just listening to the radio –weed made it all that more enjoyable. Everyone in our crew did it, but I smoked the most. I was a veritable fiend. I was stoned from sunup to sunset, 7 days a week. I know there are those among you (the more conservative of the bunch) who shudder at the mere thought, assuming marijuana is the first step on the road to ruin. But of all the bad things that can befall you, when you've decided to dedicate yourself to a life of smoking weed, I would have to say the worst one is –running out.

Not that marijuana withdrawal is anything compared to heroin tremors, alcohol shakes, nicotine fits, or even switching to decaf, but it can be bothersome.

You become depressed, listless, moody, and suddenly remember why you started smoking weed in the first place –because life sucks. Yeah, maybe for that select few (the rich and famous) life is an adventure, but for the average joe, working a nine to five, life is anything but. So you turn to drugs: caffeine, tobacco, cocaine, cannabis, alcohol, meth amphetamine, psychedelic mushrooms, nutmeg; who the fuck knows?

Not to mention the fact that buying weed is always such a hassle. Drug dealers are notorious for never answering their phone when you need them. And nothing sends chills down a stoner's spine quicker than realizing one is almost out of weed. A sense of anxiety grips you. What if I can't get a hold of my dealer tonight? Worse yet, what if I can't find anything for a couple of days? And still worse, what if the entire city is in the grip of a dry spell? What will I do to stave off the boredom and monotony of a sober life? Oh, the horror! The agony! If you've never been an addict, of any sort, you probably don't understand. But nothing gives you that warm sense of security, and well being, like an amply stocked stash box.

Sure, I had been through the DARE (Drug Abuse Resistance Education) program when I was a kid. I had seen Nancy Reagan's pasty white ass on TV telling me to, "just say no". But Nancy Reagan never had to worry about paying the rent, or living pay check to pay check, or finding her dad's rolling papers on the shelf above the coco-puffs. So I guess in Nancy Reagan's world it was pretty damn easy to adopt retarded slogans like, "just say no". I wouldn't know, though. I lived in the real world. I had problems.

At any rate, I packed the pipe, put a lighter to the bowl, and took a long hit. The first high of the day was always the best. The subsequent highs were just buzzes, more or less. I hadn't smoked since before work, so the high was decent. As I walked back out into the living room I was greeted by Horatio and Trevon (two of the guys that made up our circle of friends). They had come over to Roo and Leah's so they could follow us and Carlos to the theatre.

Carlos had been my best friend all through high school and it was him who initiated me into Tucson's elfin hip-hop community. All through school we had spent countless hours in his room (wearing Hilfiger jeans and Timberland boots), smoking weed, learning how to beat-juggle and listening to breakbeat, underground hip-hop, and rare groove records on his Technic 1200's. I'd pick him up for school everyday and on the weekends we would go to old record stores and thrift shops to "crate dig". I had always been somewhat of a loner, but Carlos was friends with all the hip-hop heads. He knew all the M.C.'s, break-dancers, graff artists and DJs in town. I don't think there was a b-boy he didn't know. It was through him that I was inducted into our little group of friends, and through him that I came to meet Roo.

Carlos used to spin hip-hop at this little club downtown every Thursday night called, The Pub. That's where we originally met Leah and Roo a few months earlier. Leah was your stereotypical downtown denizen. She had brown sun-kissed skin and was usually seen wearing sandals, oversized bangle bracelets, large earrings, gypsy skirts and Mexican peasant blouses. She had cherries tattooed on both of her shoulders, a pot belly, and rarely did anything with her hair (which was starting to form tiny little dreads). In short, she had the general appearance of a hippie.

It took her a month of hanging around the D.J. booth before Carlos finally succumbed to her advances. He kept saying she wasn't his style and he didn't go for chicks with a potbelly, but two weeks after their initial date he moved in with her and they had been together ever since. I don't know, maybe he was tired of sleeping on his dad's couch.

Carlos was a burn-out of epic proportions. He had never had a formal job, or graduated high school. Hell, he didn't even know how to drive. Some people might call a guy like this a loser. But he was my friend, my best friend. And no matter what, we had each other's back. Or so I thought.

Naturally, after Carlos started shacking up with Leah I became a regular fixture at her and her roommate's place (a little brick casita with green trimming), downtown. Truth be told, I never cared much for Leah –pot belly aside. I think she was too domineering for Carlos. Carlos' downfall, was he was too sensitive and easily influenced (he never had a mother to nurture him). Leah was simply too strong willed for him in my opinion. She would boss him around and generally treat him like her bitch. It was a sad sight.

I also thought she was somewhat of a pretentious fake. She was always championing some new movement or cause, only to abandon it as soon as a new one arrived on the scene. One week it would be the Zapatistas in Chiapas, the next week greenhouse gases, next the plight of the albino pygmy lobsters in northern Kalamazoo. It was all too insincere.

Adding to this was Leah's peculiar manner of speaking. She was Mexican by way of Colorado yet she talked like a stereotypical valley girl from California. It was all very strange. She was what we from the south-side of Tucson would refer to as a coconut. Brown on the outside, but white in the middle.

Her roommate, Roo, was a different matter altogether. She was artsy and hip with a tiny ruby stud piercing in her nose. She liked to drink Mickey's malt liquor and buy her clothes at thrift stores. She dug underground hip-hop and old-school soul. Yet, she was more conservative than she might appear at first glance. Her mother was a teacher and her father (who everyone lovingly referred to as "the colonel") was (you guessed it) a colonel in the navy; and we were the only two in our little group of friends whose parents were still married. Which, when you think about it, really isn't such a big surprise.

I mean, our generation's parents had divorced in record numbers. We were the bastard children of Nintendo and Sega. We slept together before we were married, didn't really believe in God, and had seen the birth of the computer. We were cynical, hopeless, and frustrated. We were Generation X –the unknown.

At any rate, Roo was from San Diego and only in Tucson to go to the university. But she wasn't the typical spoiled little college bitch from out of town. She was smart and witty. She had depth and character.

The worst thing about living in Tucson was everyone seemed to be from somewhere else. Native Tucsonans were a rare breed. It seemed we were infested with people from other states. The ones from back East were the worst. They constantly bitched about how backwards and behind the times Arizona was; as if we asked them to come here. They crowded our streets and polluted our air. Not to mention, they were loud and obnoxious. Rude and arrogant. They always had this superior air to them, but they were all fucking talk. They'd make a big scene and gesture a lot, but for the most part it was all hot air. Arizonans, on the other hand, are infused with the wild west mentality. We may not say as much, but we're more likely to skin our smoke-wagon and fire three hip-shots into your belly, while slamming down a shot of whiskey. We're about actions, not words. We're a bunch of little Clint Eastwoods.

Anyway, after hanging out at Leah and Roo's on a regular basis, one thing lead to another, and one night after multiple beers and mutual flirting, me and Roo ended up having sloppy drunken sex. After that, I guess you could say, we were pretty much a couple.

Talk about a relief!

It was the end of an 8 month dry spell, for me. My longest ever. Thankfully I was drunk and lasted more than two pumps before I blasted my load. To tell you the truth, I was starting to worry I might never get laid again. I had been masturbating daily for months. Sometimes twice a day. It's hard to get laid when all you do is go home and get stoned after work. Unfortunately, being a stoner and a ladies' man don't usually go hand in hand. Honestly, I was just happy to have someone to fuck.

Don't get me wrong, Roo was cool and fun to hang out with: she had big juicy tits, thin waspy lips, baby blue eyes, and dirty blond hair. But despite all this, in my heart, I felt I could do better. I mean, sometimes Roo looked kind of frumpy and unkept and I was actually embarrassed to be seen with her. She also had the habit of walking around all day in sandals, till her feet were black with filth, then hopping into bed at night without even washing her feet. It grossed me out (I have this thing about feet being clean). Plus, I was constantly wondering if she was pretty enough. I mean, she was attractive, but at this point in my life (more than anything) I wanted a woman to add to my prestige. I thought, perhaps, that a beautiful woman could repair the flaws in my character. The fractures in my self-esteem. Make me complete.

And as if all that wasn't enough. Adding to this constant inner turmoil was this beautiful seventeen year old nymphet at work – Rainy Dawn Rusch.

She was like the girl from Ipanema: tall and tan and young and lovely. She made Roo look like a straight-up dog. But she was a little cock tease. Always tempting me with her slender curves and never delivering the goods. She was 6 feet tall, with golden ringlets, light freckles, legs to her neck, and large, firm, tear shaped breasts.

Oh! I almost forgot.

Her neck!

She had the most beautiful neck. It was long and sleek like a giraffe (I have a thing for necks and shoulders). All the guys at work wanted her, so she flirted with all of us, and used her sexuality to her benefit –the little coquette. She absolutely reveled in her new found status. You could tell she wasn't used to getting this kind of attention at school. She was too tall and exotic to be appreciated by the average feeble minded high school male. But to the pack of sexual predators I worked with at McKipson's super market, she was a virtual goddess. My loins burned for her. Yet, at the same time, she was an object of constant consternation.

What can I say? I had seen her in the store at least a hundred times, shopping with her mom, before she ever started working at McKipson's. And I knew from the second I saw her, she had to be mine.

Sure, she was young, but I didn't give a shit, she was beautiful. Plus, I had just finished reading *Lolita* , so I liked to imagine she was the Dolores Hayes to my Humbert Humbert. I'd stand behind the deli counter and just watch her, like a lion watching a gazelle. Then I would think how unfair life was. How unfair, that I would never have a girl like that to share my life with. Her weekly visits became the highlight of my days.

I don't know why I was so infatuated with her. OK, maybe I do, she was fucking hot! She was every girl I had fantasized about in high school, but not been cool, or confident, enough to get. It was like she had stepped out of one of my wet dreams, or better yet, as if God had asked me to describe the most beautiful woman to him and then created her for me. But that was all physical shit, that crap only gets you so far, after that you're stuck with the person, the personality, and Rainy definitely needed some serious help in that department, I would come to find out.

I mean, other than thinking she was gorgeous I didn't know shit about her. We had never spoken, as far as I could tell she didn't even know I fucking worked there. Then one day that all changed.

It was the beginning of summer and the store was hiring like mad for the season, other than that it was like any other day. I showed up high, walked around the store a bit (looking for a snack to steal), and just when I was about ready to head back to the deli –it happened.

There she was! Rainy! Bagging groceries!

It was like a dream. I couldn't believe my eyes. I decided to ask Hector what was going on. Hector (the world's oldest bag-boy, as I liked to call him) was this 72 year oldman that bagged groceries at the store. He had retired, from some menial job or another, which of course didn't provide for it's employees golden years, so he was only working till his medi-care kicked in, in a couple years. He knew everything that went down in the store, and I used him as my constant news source. If it was McKipson's related, he knew the score.

It turned out that since Rainy's mom spent so much fucking time and money in the store, she had come to know Andy (the store manager) pretty well. As a result Andy hired Rainy on her 17th birthday, as sort of a personal favor, to her mom. I shit myself in disbelief. Were the gods finally smiling down on Vincente Vasquez?

Days passed before I could work up the nerve to go over and strike up a conversation with her. I was scared as all hell of her rejection. Nothing is worse than when a girl you like pulls the plug on your ass. It's easier to start up a conversation with a girl you find ugly, or one you just want to fuck. Who cares if they reject you, it doesn't hurt your feelings, you were just looking for a piece of ass. But this was different. I liked Rainy. Shit, I think I was in love with her. Or at least lust.

So finally, after about a week, I made up an excuse (under the flimsiest of pretexts) to go over and spark up a conversation with her. I think I pretended to need a price check for something. I started laying it on her real thick. I mean, I'm was using my best lines.

"So, are you new here?" I asked.

Okay, so maybe I wasn't Don Juan. But it worked. She took the bait and started flirting with me. Of course she flirted like a high school girl: a lot of hair flipping and arm touching, but watch out. In a few years I was certain she would be a full-blown man-eater, bending men to her will. The only reason I stood a chance now was because I had a few years on her. I knew the game a little better. But give her another four years and she'd eat me whole and spit out the seeds.

Hell, in a few years, she wouldn't even take a look at a schmoe like me. By then she would be out of my league. Right now was the only opportunity I would have with a girl like this. I currently had more to offer than any of those little high school morons that tried to pick up on her. I had a car, a decent apartment, and an unlimited supply of weed and booze. In the realm of teenage-dom this made me a god. But in a few years I would be a clown behind a deli counter. So needless to say, I decided to strike while the iron was hot and let the chips fall where they may.

What a fool.

Chapter 3
(September)

After watching *A Clockwork Orange* the gang decided to head down to The Clove Garden, it was this bar downtown that we all regularly frequented. Leah tended bar there while Roo occasionally worked the door. All the bohemian types, hip-hop heads, aspiring poets, artists and downtown denizens constantly circulated in and out of this place. It was a real den of phonies.

Yeah, I said it!

You see, although I was nearly a card carrying member of this downtown, counter culture world, I never truly felt like I fit in. I felt more like a kid staring through a knothole in a fence. Or a wildlife documentarian living amongst the apes. I found most of the people who hung out downtown to be pretentious fakes (being different merely for the sake of being different, never realizing everyone is conforming in some way). They were like Leah. Always jumping on some new cause. I never understood taking up a cause. I was too worried about saving my own ass. Maybe I was the biggest phony of all. Both drawn and repelled to this environment.

I'll have to admit, the movie had been pretty cool, though. That is to say, it was everything I didn't hate. As a matter of fact, it had so impressed me, that I went around referring to everyone as my "droogie" for at least a month. By the end I think everyone was ready to strangle me.

That night we drank until we were drunk, and then the whole crew went back to Leah and Roo's place, and smoked weed and listened to music until 3 in the morning. I woke up the next day, in Roo's bed, with a tiny demolition crew residing in my brain. The sun coming through the blinds was like the voice of god. Roo laid next to me, her nakedness exposed to the world. I couldn't recall most of the night before. I had had way too much to drink. But didn't we eventually forget everything anyway?

Chapter 4
(September)

The next day at work was a real bummer. Not only was I hung-over, but right off the bat I got called into the manager's office. It turned out that the sorority girl called the store, last night when she got home, and complained about the *wonderful* customer service I had provided her with. I guess this bitch had an axe to grind and nothing better to do. I stepped into the office and prepared for the worst. Andy, the store manager, sat behind his desk with a pink write-up slip betwixt his neatly manicured fingers.

I have to be honest, I genuinely disliked Andy. He represented everything I hated in life. He was industrious and handsome. Successful and young (only four years older than me). His shirts were always nicely ironed and he never had crap stains in his underwear. He was squeaky clean to a fault. And he had this smug self-satisfied air about him that really chapped my hide. I wanted to take him outside and beat the shit out of him, but I wasn't sure I could, he was definitely in better shape than me. He was at the gym everyday at five in the morning, bench-pressing his little heart out. I don't think I had ever woken up that early.

I worked 3pm to 9pm five days a week. I had had plenty of opportunities to work my way up to assistant manager, get forty hours a week, and an earlier shift, but I didn't want to. I wanted to be at work as little as humanly possible. As long as I had enough money to pay my rent and buy weed, I was satisfied. I had no desire to move up the corporate ladder. I viewed it as certain death. Go that route, and next thing you know, you wake up one morning and find yourself married, with a wife you didn't want and a pack of screaming brats you didn't ask for. My plan was to coast through life. I figured, if I played my cards right, and didn't fall into the "family" trap, by the time I was fifty I could retire. I didn't want to work my whole life. I wasn't industrious. I didn't have my father's work ethic. I was on the path of least resistance. The way I saw it, it didn't pay to be hardworking.

Andy, on the other hand, had reached the upper echelons of grocery store society through hard work. Hard work and ass sucking, that is, but mostly ass sucking. This guy was a grade-A butt sniffer. He had his nose so far up the corporate bosses asses, you could see the shit stains on his face a mile away. He had that smarmy disingenuous smile that makes for a great politician. You could tell the guy was intelligent, but unfortunately he was completely devoid of an original thought. He was a programmed puppet spewing mindless corporate propaganda, like a fucking tape recorder. He really bought the company's bullshit philosophy. What a chump.

With a wave of his hand, he motioned to the chair in front of his desk, and asked me to have a seat.

"How you doin' Vincente?" he asked.

"Good," I said. "you know I was wondering with the holidays coming up and everything if…"

He cut me off.

"Did you help a young lady last night?" he asked.

"Andy, I help a lot of young ladies, *if you know what I mean*," I winked.

He stayed silent, staring at the write-up. My humor lost on him.

"This one said you were rude and unhelpful."

"Well, you know as well as I do, you can't please everyone. I mean some of these customers…"

He cut me off again.

"I'm here for one thing, Vincente. Do you know what that is?"

"A pay check?" I ventured.

"To make money for this company," he answered. "And I can't do that when you are constantly pissing off customers. Do I make myself clear?"

"Crystal," I replied.

"Vincente, I want you to write a letter of re-dedication, informing me on how you plan to change your current work ethic, and why I should keep you on with the company."

I could feel my temperature rising. I wanted to jump across the table and bludgeon this cock-sucker to death, with the large crystal paper weight he had sitting on his desk. "Most definitely, I'll have it on your desk in the morning," I answered.

Talk about degrading. I would have rather shoved lit matches in my dick hole than write this bullshit letter. But I needed the job. I swallowed my pride and laid it on extra thick. It went as follows:

To the powers that be,

I, Vincente Vasquez, realize with a heavy heart, I have been remiss in my duties as of late. Nay, I have been an ungrateful fiend. Here McKipson's has given me a golden opportunity, for growth and upward mobility, and what have I done? I have bitten the hand that feeds me. My lack of appreciation borders on the obscene. I am a scoundrel! A rat!

Mighty McKipson's, if you can find it in your heart, I beg you forgive this ungrateful knave, for I have sinned. Bathe me, the unclean, so that I may be pure again. I ask this as your humble servant. And if you should find it in your magnanimous heart to pardon me, I promise to tow the line. Oh do I! I have seen the errors of my ways, and I rededicate myself to you body and soul. A thousand times I repent, and swear to perform all tasks assigned to me, no matter how menial or offensive they might be.

Sincerely,

Vincente Vasquez

My snow-job worked. McKipson's allowed me to stay on as a wage-slave and keep my rank and title. Of course I was overcome with joy.

Chapter 5
(September)

That night, at the end of my shift, I decided to go up front and flirt with Rainy. She usually worked till ten and I got off at nine every night, so it gave me a whole hour to flirt with her, before she went home. She was outside rounding up shopping carts when I found her. I got into character and walked up behind her trying to be as cool as possible.

"How are things down at the high school?" I asked placing my hands on her shapely hips.

"What's up, Vinnie?" she said, slipping out of my grasp.

She was the only one I would let get away with calling me Vinnie. To everyone else I was Vincente.

"Nothing. Just thought I would take in the night air. It's a capital evening, isn't it? You know, this is the exact way the moon looks over Milan. It's absolutely stellar! No pun intended, of course."

I couldn't believe the horse shit falling from my own mouth. I desperately wanted to impress this girl.

"You've never been to Milan."

"Well, I've read about it you know, extensively. I was actually considering writing an article on inflation and it's effect on the Milanese working class."

"Are you serious?"

"I never jest about my writing."

"I didn't know you were a writer Vinnie."

"Yes, it's a minor talent. My real passion is art, though. You should let me draw you sometime."

Who was I kidding? I couldn't draw a straight line.

"That would be really cool," she exclaimed.

We walked around the parking lot, the moon shining down on us, chit-chatting, until it was time for her to leave. Her mere presence made my body tingle.

"I better get going Vinnie. I still gotta go home and finish my homework. I hafta turn in the first-draft of an original poem by tomorrow for writing class," she stopped as if suddenly having an epiphany. "Hey, do you think if I brought my poem to work tomorrow you could read it for me, and maybe give me some help."

"Of course. I'd be delighted," I said.

She threw her arms around me, excited like a child, and hugged me. Her soft ample breasts, pressed against my chest. Her hair tickled my nose. The soft smooth skin of her cheek caressed mine. I could feel a growth inside my pants. My temperature rising. My judgment clouding. I wanted to ravage this poor girl in this dingy parking lot. I tried to compose myself. I arched my back slightly to keep her from feeling, the beast now swelling between my legs. My breath was growing labored and hot. This is how the wolfman must feel before a transformation, I thought.

"Thanks, Vinnie" she said breaking our embrace, hopping into her car and driving away, escaping the lecherous beast, that was I.

I stood there lightheaded, short of breath, and intoxicated with lust. The moon was shining down on me. I threw my head back and howled.

Chapter 6
(September)

It was Thursday night and that meant one thing, and one thing only, The Pub on Pennington Street. Every Thursday night was hip-hop night at The Pub. It was a real chill place where all the hip-hop heads would congregate. There'd be M.C. battles, impromptu breaking competitions, and people just grabbing the mic and freestyling. The whole crew would get together, mob the place up, drink beer, smoke bidis, and occasionally go out to the parking lot to smoke a jay. Horatio and Trevon would usually be the first ones, of our crew, to show up rocking Oakley ski goggles and North Face bubble goose vests. These two knuckle-heads were inseparable and usually went everywhere with each other. They were so close, they had even done time together.

A couple of years prior they had gone to Hawaii. When they ran out of money half way through their trip, Horatio had come up with the brilliant idea that they burglarize a golf store, and sell the loot to rich tourists on vacation. It was the perfect plan, until they got caught selling stolen goods to an off duty officer. The judge gave them three months in the can where they acquired the nicknames Lee Trevino and Tiger Woods, respectively; on account of Horatio's Mexican, and Trevon's Black, ancestry.

What can you say? They were just a couple of guys who liked to have fun. You could usually find them on the dance floor doing the Uprock, Popping, or once in a while for a laugh the Kid 'n Play Kickstep. And every once in awhile, Trevon would even grab the mic and lay down a rhyme or two of his own.

The other two that were sure to show were Santos and Emma. Unlike most of the group, which I was newly acquainted with, I had known Santos and Emma for years. Emma and me had been going to school together since 1st grade, and Santos had started working at McKipson's the same year as me. We both started in high school as bag-boys, the only difference was Santos got fired three months later for stealing spray-paint, I unfortunately, was still there.

Santos was the epitome of a slacker. He couldn't hold a job to save his life. Maybe the hypocrisy of working a 9 to 5 was too much for him to bear. He finally had to settle for working sporadically in his father's automated laundromat. Which was a shame for someone with such talent. He was a great artist. And probably the best graff artist in town. In high school he had been in a graffiti crew with Trevon, Horatio and a few other guys called CWA (City Wide

Assault). They were the only dudes in town getting up on billboards and rocking sick-ass pieces with like 16 colors. To this day you can occasionally go into a bathroom, and see a mirror, scribed with Santos' old tag, Mad Man, in frenzied scrawl.

And that was it. That was the core of our crew (me, Roo, Carlos, Leah, Horatio, Trevon, Santos, and Emma). We were all in our early twenties and out of our minds. We drank too much, smoked weed, and popped pills. We were tattooed and pierced, listless and lazy. We were the epitome of Gen X, burn-outs.

There were other people that would hang with us, but they usually had a separate core of friends. That was the really cool thing about the downtown scene, everyone seemed to know each other by proxy. It was it's own little community. A self-sustaining bohemian microcosm. A city inside a city where the theory of six degrees of separation was considerably smaller.

After a night at The Pub we'd usually hit up the Grill. It was this conceited greasy spoon, dating back to the 1920's. And of course, since it was downtown, it was manned by a bunch of self-entitled, stuck-up, hipsters. I often wondered how the place managed to stay afloat so long with such a rude and inattentive staff. They adhered to a set of arbitrary rules like refusing to put cheese on potatoes or serve ranch dressing. And instead of helping customers, they seemed to prefer smoking cigarettes, reading dog eared copies of Vonnegut (why I don't know, I had read *Jail Bird* and failed to see the appeal), and seating their friends before "common" patrons.

But what the place lacked in service, I guess they made up for in charm. It had a great atmosphere: blood-red leather booths, scuffed linoleum floors, a vintage Formica counter with spinning stools, and a beautiful art-deco mural depicting a pale, mint-green, doe and her fawn. It was authentic kitsch. This was no franchise fabrication, it was the real deal. A living relic from a bygone age. The place even allowed you to smoke (as long as it wasn't bidis or cloves), despite a city ordinance prohibiting such acts in restaurants. And the food was pretty decent too. What foodies might call, high diner: fresh lumberjack sized breakfasts', thick sandwiches loaded with premium sliced deli meat, and real mashed potatoes with rich pork hock gravy. I guess, therein lay the secret to their success.

Luckily Leah and Roo knew most of the waitresses so we never had any problems getting service. All of us would cram into a couple of booths and commandeer the joint for a couple of hours, acting like we were the Rat Pack or something. At this time in the morning every one was either high, drunk, or both. It made for a colorful event. And although it was fun, it took some getting used to.

I was somewhat of a loner by nature, I never really cared for parties or social gatherings, and wasn't used to always hanging around so many people. I preferred more intimate gatherings of one or two friends. And Roo, knowing this, would try to accommodate me from time to time.

Every Monday was 80's night at Club Congress, yet another bar downtown, so occasionally me and Roo would ditch the crew and go there to sweat-out the days frustrations dancing to New Order, Joy Division, or Depeche Mode. Roo loved 80's new wave.

Other times we would go to the Seven Black Cats, and smoke cigarettes and drink Lone Star beer in brown glass bottles for a buck, as we told each other child-hood stories and laughed all night long.

And yet other times we'd go to the south-side, in the middle of the day, for Mexican food, or the west-side for Pat's chili dogs served with a mound of greasy fries. But my absolute favorite thing to do was break into the sandwich shop Roo worked at after hours.

The Ham on Rye was this little hole in the wall deli on 4th avenue. It was owned by Roo's friend and resident downtown drunk, Tammy

Smith. Tammy was in her late thirties and going nowhere fast. When not at the sandwich shop she could usually be found at one of the bars downtown, namely Che's Lounge or The Buffet. She lacked the work ethic needed to run a lucrative business. Half the time, she'd forget to pick up things like ham or roast beef; two things imperative to running a successful deli. And when she wasn't forgetting something she was usually showing up too hung-over to work. I guess it didn't help that her boyfriend was owner of The Clove Garden, the bar where Leah and occasionally Roo worked. The last thing a drunk needs is a bar owner for a boyfriend.

At any rate, at least once a week, me and Roo would sneak down there in the middle of the night (stoned out of our minds and suffering from a serious case of the munchies), to pillage The Ham on Rye. Seeing how Tammy was unreliable, Roo had her own set of keys, so she could open the shop whenever Tammy was too drunk to show up. It made our midnight raids a piece of cake. Once inside, we'd concoct Dagwood-esque monstrosities of: ham, turkey, cream cheese, cucumbers, mustard, spinach, and sprouts all piled on top of 12 grain bread. It was a free-for-all. One night, in one of our wilder moments, we even had stoned pot-sex on top of the prep table where they made the sandwiches. Undoubtedly, a mortal sin.

It was times like this when I was happiest with Roo, when it was just the two of us. These were the moments I could see myself maybe even falling in love with her. But in the back of my mind Rainy always resided. The idea of her. The fantasy I had created.

Chapter 7
(mid September)

Working in the deli you had to deal with all kinds of schmucks. Like little old ladies wanting a quarter pound of havarti, sliced paper thin, with a piece of wax paper between every slice, so they could peel it apart easier when they fed it to their cat, Mr. Wrinkles. Soccer moms wanting 30 lbs. of sliced boiled ham, broke down into quarter pound packages, to feed their army of snot-nosed brats. And of course, there was always the frat-boy fuck-heads ordering 80 pieces of fried chicken right before the "big game", with only an hour notice. Not to mention the myriad of other things you had to deal with on a daily basis.

But of all my friends I was the only one to have a "reliable" job. McKipson's had health insurance, a 401k plan, paid vacation, and a pension. They even paid me enough that I could afford to live on my own (I was only one, in our crew of friends, who didn't live downtown and didn't have a roommate; I lived in a modest apartment on the far east side). All McKipson's asked for in return was your soul.

My friends thought I had it made, though. They thought I had found the goose that laid the golden egg. They all worked unstable jobs in little downtown establishments (part time bartenders, store clerks, door-men). They were jobs with no futures. Not even the next day was guaranteed (downtown business' were highly volatile, nothing lasted more than a few years, and most less).

But what my friends didn't realize was, I found my job soul-crushing. Every day I went to work I died a little bit inside. I couldn't help but feel I wasn't living up to my full potential. At this point in my life I had yet to work anywhere besides McKipson's, but what I had come to realize from my time spent there was –people were generally lazy, myself included. The funny thing was most people thought they were hard workers.

It wasn't uncommon to be in the break room and hear employee "X" talk about how lazy employee "Y" was. Never mind the fact that employee "X" was supposed to be mopping up a jar of mayo on aisle 12, yet here he was eating stolen Twinkies in the break room. It was hypocrisy on the grandest scale. In a store of about 59 people, maybe about 6 gave a 100% everyday, the rest of us did just enough to get by. And rightfully so! The company treated us like chattel. Giving us just enough to survive. I must admit though, I admired those 6 people for their diligence, but at the same time I couldn't help but feel they were suckers. Where was their reward? My father had raised me to believe hard work would always be recognized and rewarded, but that was a crock of shit. It was the ass-suckers and weasels that made head way. Everyone else would become faceless casualties on the battlefield. Show any sign of industriousness and the company would milk you dry. Just like poor Sophia.

In 33 years of service, Sophia had never missed a day of work. She always came in early when called, or stayed late when asked. Who knows how many days off she sacrificed to cover shifts others had abandoned. She was always the first one called by managers when there was extra work to be done. Rumor had it she had once been beautiful and young. A honey skinned Aztec princess. Homecoming queen of her high school. Not anymore though. All that remained now was the discarded husk of a once beautiful woman. Her fingers resembled gnarled and knotty pieces off drift wood, and she wore braces on both wrists due to carpal tunnel acquired through years of repetitious cashiering. Her orange beehive (with it's grey roots) seemed to be a permanent fixture on register five. That is of course, until she made the mistake of slipping on a puddle of milk in the dairy cooler, while doing a price check. After that none of us ever saw her again. A get-well-soon card was passed around work and a donation taken up (Sophia lived in a shoddy trailer in a poor area of town with the three granddaughters she was raising), but that was the last I ever heard of her. Someone once told me the company was trying to screw her out of her workers comp and disability, saying that her fall was due to her own negligence. That she shouldn't have been working while, taking heart medication that could make her drowsy and screw with her equilibrium. Forget that she needed that medicine to live, that was her problem. That was the way of corporate America. That was her thanks for 33 years. I suppose it could have been worse though. She could have been Penny.

Penny was this crazy old lady, with more whiskers than a walrus, who hung-out by the dumpster behind McKipson's and pilfered throwaways: old produce, stale baked goods, out of code deli items. Her stringy gray hair was always greasy and her clothes crusted with dirt. She wore the same canvas shoes everyday, sockless and blackened with filth, and she always smelled of b.o. and urine. Most of my coworkers, although they couldn't stand her, couldn't wait to find her out back, if for no other reason, but to chase her away like an old alley cat.

I never understood it. After all, she was someone's daughter, sister, maybe mother. She never bothered anybody, she was merely looking for something to eat. Scraps that the rest of the world had discarded. I was always curious how her current state befell her. I mean, there but for the grace of God, go I. The truth is, none of us are ever more than a second away from destitution. And for that reason alone, I always tried to help her in my own little way.

Every night, before I'd take the trash out, I'd try to put something aside for her on the chance she was outside rifling through the dumpster. She never thanked me –verbally that is. Instead she'd smile a semi-toothless smile and nod. Staring at me with eyes, as warm and blue as the Mediterranean sea. Then she'd gather up all her little treasures for the evening, pile them into the wire basket she had affixed to the front of her rusty old Schwin, and pedal off (her bike swaying this way and that, under the light of the moon). It was all the thanks I ever needed.

Chapter 8
(mid September)

A couple of weeks later Rainy brought her poem to work for me to review. It was bad. No, it was beyond bad. It was worst poem *ever* – a Seussian nightmare. It made me want to gouge my eyes out and pour salt in the wounds. The worse part was she insisted that I read it, right there in front of her, while she watched me. I fought a tremendous battle to keep my face from displaying the disgust I felt inside. I could feel her icy stare searching my every nuance and twitch for meaning. It was man vs. emotion. I struggled greatly to keep my poker face on. The poem went thusly:

Love is a dove

Sent from above

And from the start

You had my heart

And when you are gone

It is your kiss

That I miss

So always stay near

I love you my dear

"So, what do you think?" she asked.

What could I tell this girl? It was like a bad greeting card. I wanted to slit my wrists with this poem.

"Not bad," I answered.

"I'm sure it's not as good as the stuff you write, but I think I did alright."

"No. No, it's great," I assured her.

"So, should I change anything? I hafta turn in the final draft next week," she said.

How many times did this chick want me to lie? Was she fucking with me?

"Well, why don't you let me take it home and think about it. Poems need to resonate with me sometimes," I said.

"Yeah, that would be awesome," she said. "Thanks Vinnie."

She put her arms around me and gave me a strong lingering hug. I melted.

My next day off I woke up early, smoked a joint, and sat down with Rainy's poem. I read it over and over again, and each time it got worse. I wanted to help her fix it, but I didn't know how. I had never written a poem. I had never written anything. I only knew that hers was bad.

I decided to just write the whole thing over, and try to keep as faithful to the source material as possible. And to my surprise it all came together.

love like

a white

bird

or a

fallen piece

of heaven

you

creating

a coronary

ache

I am

a waif

in need

of your

touch

your

warmth

stay

I couldn't tell if it was any good or not, but I knew it was a hell of a lot better than the original. At least all that corny rhyming was gone. And I was shocked at how easy it had come to me. I didn't even have to think about it. The words just came out. I took it to work the next day eager to please Rainy.

It seemed like forever till Rainy showed up the next day. I kept looking towards the break-room every few minutes to make sure I hadn't missed her coming in. Finally, after an anxiety ridden eternity, she arrived.

She had come directly from school and was still wearing her street clothes –some painted on jeans with a tight white top that exposed her mid-riff. If you looked closely enough, you could see the barely visible blond peach fuzz that made up her happy-trail. It was like the fabled yellow brick road, starting at the piercing in her navel, and ending at the holiest of holies. I grabbed the poem and made a beeline to the break-room. I found her there alone, fumbling with the combination to her locker.

"Hey, I brought your poem back," I said coming up from behind.

"Awesome!" she said spinning around and snatching it from my fingers.

"I took some liberties with it," I said sheepishly. "I hope you don't mind."

She just looked down at the poem, then at me, then at the poem again.

"I mean, it's still all there. The essence, you know. I just changed some of the words."

She looked at me again. A vacant look across her face.

Oh, shit!

I had done it this time. There was no way this girl was ever gonna let me bang her, now. I had butchered her poem. Why couldn't I just leave well enough alone? I was certain she would slap me at any moment, but instead she spoke.

"It's magical," she said.

"Really," I asked in disbelief. "you think?"

"Oh, yes. I could never write like this. It's beautiful," she exclaimed.

"Well, yes," I said in new found confidence. "as I said, writing is a minor talent of mine, you know."

"No, this is really good," she said.

Here was my opportunity. The in I had been waiting for.

"Well, your words touched me deeply. I was inspired. That poem is all you though," I said. "You created it. I merely breathed a little life into it. But it was your strong foundation which allowed me to."

"Thank you," she said kissing me deeply on the lips.

Chapter 9
(October)

Fall is my favorite time of year. The morning air is always cool and crisp, it seems to invigorate one, making you feel as if anything is possible. It's like nature's aftershave, clean and biting. Sometimes, early in the morning, you'll see a family of javelina crossing the road, or a lone coyote returning home from his nightly excursion. I always feel more like myself in the fall (if you could call what we experience here, truly fall, it's better explained as a softening of the heat, the days are in the 80's and the nights the mid 50's). The angst and dread that usually grips me is replaced by a quiet gray longing, and a sort of bittersweet melancholy overtakes me. I'm more apt to spending time alone with my thoughts –reviewing the year, before the hustle and bustle of the holiday season.

Soon, it will be time for the annual migration of the snowbirds. Like the swallows to Capistrano these faithful birds return every year to the Arizona desert, retirement checks in hand. If you are unfortunate enough, you might catch glimpse of a saggy-breasted-blue-hair in your local grocery store. Or while at the movies you may spot a group of liver-spotted-cane-wobblers. And of course the wandering-dementia-dodos are always abundant.

Yes, October and her autumn kiss had finally arrived. And naturally, change was in the air (both good and bad) –there was no denying it.

Roo and Leah were planning a Halloween party and I wanted nothing to do with it (and surprisingly neither did Carlos). As I've said, I never cared for parties. The bowl of chips. The mindless small talk with strangers. Someone puking in the bushes. I preferred my gatherings small and intimate. But Roo and Leah were hell bent on inviting as many people as they could. I was pretty sure half of downtown would be there. They said if me and Carlos didn't want to get in the spirit we didn't have to come. We could go be party poopers somewhere else.

Excellent I thought, this was the perfect opportunity for me to creep on Rainy while Roo was preoccupied. Carlos eventually folded like a chair and attended the party. I spent the evening elsewhere, chasing Rainy.

Chapter 10
(late October)

That weekend one of the cashiers from up front was throwing a Halloween party. Usually I wouldn't have been caught dead within a hundred miles of the damn thing, but this time was different. I saw this as a prime opportunity to put the moves on Rainy.

Ever since our kiss in the break-room I had been thinking about her incessantly. Rainy on the other hand had been kind of aloof. She said she knew I had a girlfriend and that she shouldn't have kissed me. That it wasn't right. I told her not to worry because she was the one I really wanted to be with, and that I wasn't even into Roo. When she asked why I hadn't broke up with her yet then, I didn't know what to say.

I mean, in my heart I knew the reason, but I couldn't tell Rainy why. The reason was I was scared of being alone. Those eight months I had spent by myself, before getting with Roo, were some of the loneliest times I have ever had. I truly started to believe I would be alone for the rest of my life. Here I was, only 22, and I thought no one would ever love me again. Suicide started to seem like a comforting possibility. I found it reassuring that no matter how bad things got there was always a way out. It takes a certain type of melancholy boy to believe such a thing. Maybe it was the weed, I don't know.

The only real friend I had during this whole turbulent time was my cousin Mona. She's a year older than me and has always been somewhat of a surrogate big sister to me. Before Roo it was Mona who would drag me out to eighties night at Club Congress or The Cage in an attempt to help me forget my woes, even if it was only for a few hours. Every time we'd go though, deep in my heart, I would secretly hope to meet somebody who really loved me. But failing to do so, I would go home even more depressed, and want to die. It was nights like this Mona would allow me to fall asleep on her couch, crying. And although we weren't hanging out as much as we used to (she had recently moved in with her putz boyfriend), I'm certain I wouldn't have made it through that tumultuous time without her.

At any rate, I showed up to the Halloween party without a costume. Automatically I stood out like a sore thumb. Here I was surrounded by all manner of ghost, goblin and spook, and I was wearing a pair of baggy jeans and a hoody. Talk about a faux pas.

I didn't see Rainy anywhere around, so I made my way to the back porch and the coolers filled with beer; making sure I said "What's up?" to everyone I passed and trying desperately to fit in. Most of these people I only knew casually. It's not like I was the most sociable fellow.

I fished two beers out of the ice and slammed them back to back. Within a few minutes I started to feel better. The voices inside my head started to chill out a bit. I grabbed another beer, made my way back inside to the kitchen, and started chatting up a group of Mexican girls from the bakery (with the alcohol coursing through my system I was no longer so self-conscious). They were dressed like a sexy cop, a nurse, and a maid. I never understood why girls

Halloween costumes were always slutty versions of regular things. I thought it was funny. Why weren't guys costumes like that? When the bakery girls asked what I was supposed to be, I said, "A pervert." They all laughed.

Then, in the middle of the laughter, as if planned by God himself, Rainy walked in dressed like Tinkerbell. She looked absolutely scrumptious in her little green dress and gossamer wings. All the guys stared in awe. I couldn't have asked for things to work out any better. I could see the twinkling of jealousy in Rainy's eyes when she saw me surrounded by three hot girls. It must have took every ounce of her strength to push it down inside herself and make her way to me.

"Vinnie," she said hugging me. "I didn't expect to see you here."

"Well, I came just for *you*," I said.

The bakery girls just gave her a catty look and went back to talking amongst themselves.

"Come out back with me,' Rainy said pulling my arm.

Out back a photo shoot was in full swing. Roberta, the woman throwing the party accosted both of us on sight.

"Hey you two, get your asses over here! We're taking a picture. Vincente, where the fuck is your costume?"

Roberta was a short brassy gal that looked like she put her makeup on with a paint-ball gun. She was dressed like a witch and she was already drunk.

"I forgot it was Halloween," I said.

"Whatever, you two get your tall asses and stand in the back."

We made our way to the back. When we got there Rainy stood behind me and rested her chin on my shoulder; making sure to push her soft ample breasts into the back of my arm. It was the exact kind of thing you would expect a high school girl to do.

After the picture I slammed a couple more beers and bullshitted with the guys a bit, while Rainy chatted with the girls. I was starting to feel pretty good. And from the look of things, so was Rainy. She was talking louder than usual and using her hands to express herself, a clear sign that she was feeling the effects of the wine-coolers she was drinking. I decided to make my move. I grabbed a couple of beers and asked her to go out to the front yard with me.

It was a chilly night and the sky was completely black. I offered her my sweat-shirt and she took it. It fit her big and she seemed to swim around in it. I gave her one of the beers. She opened it and took a drink, making a face as she did, I could tell she wasn't accustomed to the taste of beer.

"Taste good?" I asked.

"Not really," she said. "but it does what it is supposed to do."

I lead her down the car lined street to where I had parked my car. When we got to my car we leaned our backs against it and looked up at the starry sky.

"I was really surprised to see you tonight. I didn't think you liked these kind of things," she said.

"I told you, I only came to see you," I answered.

"Really?"

"Yeah."

She looked down at her feet as if thinking.

"What about your girlfriend?" she asked.

"What girlfriend," I said.

I moved so I was standing in front of her and started kissing her. She didn't stop me. Instead, she kissed me back. After a couple of minutes it started to get hot. The beer had given me a false sense of courage. So, I slid my right hand up and squeezed her breast. She shoved her tongue deeper into my mouth. In response, I pushed my erect dick into her thigh and kissed her harder. She started to make little moaning noises. I could hardly believe what was happening. I was giddy with joy. The adrenalin coursed through my veins.

"Let's get in the backseat of my car," I said.

"I can't do that."

"Yeah, come on."

"Just keep kissing me," she said rubbing my dick through my pants.

After a couple of more minutes and a few more failed attempts to get her in my car, I broke away frustrated.

"I better get going. It's getting late," I said.

She stood there fixing her costume. Straightening her hair.

"Alright, I better get back to the party anyway, I know people are in there gossiping away. Here is my number though. Call me tomorrow."

She pulled a small piece of paper out of her little purse, scribbled down her number, and stuffed it in my hand. She gave me one more tiny kiss then started to walk back to the party.

"I'm glad you came tonight," she shouted over her shoulder.

"Me too," I shouted back.

I watched her disappear into the darkness, my eyes fixated on her ass the whole time.

Chapter 11
(early November)

The next couple of weeks were kind of strange. I spent my days juggling my time between Roo and Rainy. While Roo was at work during the day I'd go over to Rainy's house and spend the mornings with her, before I had to go to work and she to school (it was Rainy's senior year so she only had half a day and didn't have to be in school till noon). We had hung out everyday since the party. We'd lay on her mother's couch and spoon while watching movies, and make-out all morning. I lied and told her I had broke up with Roo in hope we might get together, but I'm not sure she believed me. I think that's the reason she was hesitant to make us an official item and let me fuck her.

I mean, we would fool around and stuff, but we had yet to consummate this strange symbiosis we shared. I decided to follow Hector's advice and try going down on her.

Hector (the world's oldest bag-boy) had been married four times and seen a lot of shit, so he liked to give us young guys advice, especially about women.

He told me this story once, about how when he was young, there was this fat little redhead he was trying to bang. She'd let him get her butt-naked and squeeze her fat tits and finger her chubby pussy all the time, but she would never let him seal the deal. It made me laugh to imagine skinny-ass Hector, in his baggy socks, rolling around and trying to get it on with this chunky little redhead.

Anyway, after weeks of this frustration, he finally decided to try something new and drop on this chick. He said he must have given her the lick-job of a lifetime, because after that she was like putty in his hands. He could fuck her all he wanted. After hearing about my problems with Rainy, he suggested I try this proven technique. I figured, why not give it a try? Someone as old as Hector, surely had to know what they were talking about, right?.

So, the next time I was at Rainy's house and things started to get hot and heavy, I suavely slid her pants down, placed my head between her legs, and began to lap. She squirmed and moaned in ecstasy. I swear, I must have went down on her for like an hour. My jaw was sore for a week and I was picking pubes out of my teeth the rest of the day. She must of cummed seven or eight times. Afterwards I thought, "this is it, I'm finally gonna get some". I could feel my member throbbing in anticipation. I rolled over on my back, started to unbuckle my pants, and prepared to enter Rainy's heavenly pink crevice. But all of a sudden I heard a commotion to the left of me. Rainy was standing up, sliding her pants back on, and fixing her hair.

"You better get going," she said. "I gotta go to school."

"What!" I said. "School?!"

I stood up in disbelief, my pants sliding down around my ankles. My penis going flaccid.

"Yeah, school" she said casually.

I couldn't believe it. Were the gods against me? Was I the biggest loser alive? I gathered up what little self-esteem I had left and headed for the door. Rainy gave me a peck on the lips and told me to call her later. I went home a broken and defeated man. Goddamn, Hector!

Chapter 12
(mid November)

Things went on like this for a couple of weeks. And I must admit, even though Rainy wasn't fucking me, I was pretty happy. I liked living a double life –mornings with Rainy and evenings with Roo. And although it was tiring at times (trying to keep two women happy and all), somehow I managed. How some men managed to juggle more than two women is beyond me. I mean, there are men out there with modern day harems, god bless them. Two was enough for me. But, as they say, all good things must come to an end.

After work, one night, I headed over to Roo's place. I wanted nothing more, than to get high and forget the day (my job was really getting to me, I wasn't sure how much longer I could last). When I got there I was surprised to find all the lights off; from the outside it appeared no one was home. I decided to try the front door. Curiously it was unlocked. I let myself in.

I crept around the house uncertain of what was going on. I half expected a burglar to jump out. Carlos and Leah were no where to be found, but I could see a light coming from underneath Roo's bedroom door. I mentally prepared myself for a fight and walked in uncertain of what I was going to find. To my shock it was only Roo. She was laying on her bed, eyes blood shot, with a half smoked joint lying on the night stand next to her.

I quickly felt the trepidation I felt moments earlier, turning into indignation. Was she smoking my weed with out me? I had recently started keeping a stash there, on the account of us spending so much time together.

"Is that my weed?" I asked.

She peered up as if taking note of me for the first time. Her eyes were sunk in and her skin had an ashy tone to it. She looked like a ghost. Like something terrible had happened.

"My sister is dead," she said beginning to weep.

I sat down on the bed next to her and stared at the floor. Examining the minute details in the wood grain. The flecks of dirt. The dust bunny in the corner. I didn't know what to say.

Chapter 13
(mid November)

Niki (Roo's sister) had been a drinker for years. And for the most part she had been so unscathed. I mean, she had two D.U.I.'s and had done a stint in a recovery program (under her parent's authority), but for the most part nothing horrendous had happened. Then one night her luck ran out.

She had been out with some of the girls from work enjoying a few cocktails, and everything seemed perfectly normal. They talked about guys, what a prick their boss was, and shamelessly flirted with the bartender. She wondered if she had a clean skirt to wear to work the next day and whether or not the cat had enough food at home. It was like any other night. The moon was out and the stars twinkled, and all over the country children were being nestled into their beds. Everything was as it had always been. Then around 11:30 p.m. they all said goodbye, got in their cars and parted ways. The next morning Niki's car was found wrapped around a telephone pole while her chest was found crushed by a steering column. She had died on the spot from internal bleeding, leaving behind a pair of grieving parents and an emotionally distraught sister.

Roo had always looked up to her sister. As a matter of fact, she idolized her. Niki was five years older than her and a constant source of inspiration. As a kid, Roo would try to dress, talk, and tease her hair out like Niki. She even went as far as to co-opt her sister's taste in music (*The Smiths* and *The Cure*). They were as close as two sisters could be. They'd talk on the phone twice a week and e-mail each other regularly.

At the time of her death, Roo's sister had been living in San Diego where they had grown up. Their father had been stationed there when they were children and Niki had always loved it. She couldn't imagine living anywhere else. The Colonel and Roo's mom had since moved to sunny Florida to retire, and they decided that's where Roo's sister should be buried, as well. That way they could be close to her.

But before that could happen, Roo had to go to San Diego to clean out her sister's apartment before her parents got there. It was her job to make sure she got rid of any incriminating evidence like dildos, booze, drug paraphernalia, or any other embarrassing items a grieving parent shouldn't have to look at (no father wants to find his dead little girl's industrial pussy plunger). She was also responsible for finding something, among her sister's personal effects, for her to be buried in. Talk about a shitty time.

I wanted to be as comforting as possible, but it was hard, Roo and I had only been going out for a few of months at this time and I was still getting to know her. Plus, I never knew what to say when someone died anyway. Sorry, never seemed to suffice. So, every night when she would call me, I would just sit and listen, trying to be supportive as possible, but never really saying much.

To make things even more complicated, it turned out Roo's sister and her boyfriend had been getting pretty close. Close enough to be talking marriage. He had even gone as far as to buy the ring, and he had been planning to pop the question that weekend.

I suppose all of this wouldn't have been such a big deal, if any of Roo's family had met him before, but they hadn't. So now, this understandably distraught and blubbering guy, is asking Roo which flight she is catching to Florida, so maybe they can go together. She really wasn't into the idea, but he kept on saying how he was in no condition to be left alone, as if Roo was right as rain.

Talk about a complete fucking disaster. The last thing you should have to do when mourning is comfort your dead sister's boyfriend. Personally, I would have told the guy to fuck-off. But out of respect for her dead sister, Roo reluctantly let the schmuck tag along. Poor girl. Meanwhile, I had my own problems.

Chapter 14
(mid November)

It was time for the store's quarterly meeting. Every three months McKipson's had a pow-wow. It was middle-management's opportunity to tell us how much money we had made for Tommy McKipson, and how much we were expected to make for him next quarter. Now if your not from Arizona you've probably never heard of Tommy McKipson, so allow me to elaborate. Good ol' Tommy is some what of a local celebrity. He's the only son of Irish immigrants, and the sole heir to a grocery store chain rumored to be worth millions. But Tom's aspirations reach far beyond double coupon Thursday. Not only does he own a chain of grocery stores, but he's also a failed politician. About six years ago he had made a play for the governor's seat, unfortunately for him, to no avail. Since then he had spent most of his time looking for tax breaks, monopolizing the grocery business in the South West, and squashing any chance for his company to be voted into the union. Yeah, he was a real man of the people.

At any rate, I was fifteen minutes early and the room was already half full. All the brown-nosers had decided to show up early and get a head start on their apple polishing. I was early because since birth my father had drilled punctuality into me. That and because I was high and wanted to sneak in before too many people showed up. The thing about being high is, you're always worried people can tell, and that they will blow your cover. I wanted to get a seat in back, away from everybody, and let my high wear-off a bit before I had to interact with anyone. Anyway, these weren't bad people. They didn't mean to be such ass kissers. They were just victims of the system. Faceless cogs scared of losing their job. Monkeys lost to the machine.

I was pretty sure it was like this everywhere. People giving a song and dance to keep a job they hated. Busting their backs and asses trying to give their kids what they never had. I had seen too many people destroyed this way. Namely my father. No wonder he was always pissed-off and beating my ass. The 9 to 5 gives a man no time to live. It's a con-game. They give you just enough to keep you hungry. Just enough to make you think you are doing better than your parents before you. But in reality it's a lie. We stay poor while the rich get richer. The horses run over the hills, the sky shines blue, and life goes on as it always has.

So there I was, sitting in the back of the local Elks lodge (that's where they held these meetings), wondering how it came to this. Wondering where I went wrong in life. Wondering how a proletariat is born. It was going a be a long night. The shitty thing was Rainy wouldn't even be there to flirt with. She was only a bagger and they weren't required to attend these meetings. I guess the company didn't view them as elemental to our success.

Up front, distanced from us "common" workers, as always, sat Andy and the department heads. They sat there thanking God for not making them one of us. One of the grunts. A piss ant. They thought they were so much better than us regular slobs because they got to wear a gold vest, instead of a green apron. What a joke! Is this what society had come to? Stooges vying for a colored vest. Didn't they realize it was just a scam perpetrated by the CEO's to pit us against each other. A trick to enable them to control us better.

Hell, management was just as expendable as us, if not more so, after all, they're the ones who made all the money. Got the five week vacations. The full coverage benefits. The bonuses. When a company downsizes, or gets bought out, and they eventually all do, who do they think is going to get the axe first? Sally jockeying the register at $7.50 an hour? I don't think so. Most places trim their fat from the top. These managers didn't have a clue.

The room slowly started to fill. Some car pooled, some came alone, and still others brought their kids. The kids ran around, made noise, farted, spilt soda, and did pretty much anything else their little heart's desired. They had yet to be captured. Broken. They ran wild believing the center of the earth was made of cotton candy and that only good things would happen to them. They had yet to hear of taxes, mortgages, unexpected doctor bills, and all the other treats life has in store for one. A clipboard went around and we all signed in. Then it was time for the meeting to begin.

Andy told us the gross profit, the labor costs, shrink, and a bunch of other stuff no one cared about. Then it was time for a special treat! A word from Tommy McKipson himself. The store manager popped a tape into the VCR and Tommy came to life in all his Technicolor glory. He sat in a big chair with an American flag draped behind it. A sullen look was plastered across his face. He looked like the president does when he gets on TV and announces that we have just gone to war.

"Friends," he started. "let me begin by saying, thank you for all your hard work and dedication, because it's YOU, that makes McKipson's what it is today. For the last seven years we've recorded a gross annual profit of thirty-five percent. And frankly friends, that's nothing to snub your noses at."

Andy began to clap. His toadies followed suit. Before I knew it everyone was clapping. I look around confused. Why were they clapping? We hadn't seen a penny of that money. As a matter of fact the company had just rescinded another paid holiday –Easter. Hell, if you couldn't get a paid day off for a man coming back from the dead, what could you get one for? I noticed Andy looking at me. I decided I better play along. I was in enough trouble. I clapped my hands and nodded my head in approval like everyone else.

Tommy went on.

"But unfortunately friends, were about to fall on troubled times. For years now we've reigned as the undisputed king of the jungle, but there is a new lion in town, and what is about to happen can only be described as a Nazi blitzkrieg. It's like the invasion of Poland all over again." Tommy paused. It was as if what he was about to say was too painful for him.

Wow, I thought. This must really be something bad.

Tommy collected himself and continued.

"In the next six months, Wal-Mart," he said with a look of disgust on his face. "intends on opening three new mega-marts in town."

What!! I couldn't believe my ears. Had he just compared the opening of a few grocery stores to World War II? I was a little perturbed by this analogy. Everyone else watched the television intently. As if some great truth was about to be told.

"But I'm certain, with your hard work and dedication, not only will we pull through, but we will defeat this evil enemy!"

The room exploded in applause. People stamped their feet and hollered. I couldn't believe what I was seeing. They were completely brainwashed. What did we care if Wal-Mart took over and McKipson's went belly-up. It was merely a changing of the guards as far as I was concerned. Replacing one evil master with another. I'd get a job at Wal-Mart, buy my six-pack, watch TV, and life would go on as it always had. I had no loyalty to Tommy McKipson. As he had none to me. It was a dog eat dog world.

Tommy looked down at his desk reflectively. Then continued. The room fell silent.

"There is only one thing that troubles me friends."

They hung on his every word. Dogs waiting for a bone.

"There are some among you, who feel compelled to shop elsewhere. To turn their backs on the company that has bought their homes and fed their families. The company that has done so much for them. And do you know why they do this friends? I'll tell you. They do this in the name of saving a few cents."

People looked at the person next to them. Everyone was a suspect. I decided I better do the same. I glared at all of them. Managers, kids, the stuffed elk heads hanging on the wall. Benedict Arnold's, every one of them.

But the truth was, I couldn't afford to shop at McKipson's. Like everyone else I was on a budget, and McKipson's was the most expensive store in town. I mean, if I shopped there, where would I get money for drugs and booze?

Tommy went on.

"As far as I'm concerned, if you can't be bothered to shop where you work, than you're a TRAITOR! A FILTHY TRAITOR! And at McKipson's we have no use for TRAITORS!"

Again the room exploded. This time it came unglued. A deafening applause filled the air. Everyone was trying to out do the person next to them. Trying to prove their loyalty. Andy stood up front looking around the room. Making sure everyone was in accordance.

"Shit," I thought. "I better do something quick."

I jumped up, knocked over my chair, and shouted Hallelujah! in feigned joy. Others followed my lead. Someone up front fainted. A woman in back wept. I wanted to puke. It was a sickening sight.

"Jesus Christ," I thought. " Where's George Orwell when you need him?"

It took about five minutes to get everyone to settle down, and by then the meeting was supposed to be over. They paid us by the hour for these things, so management hated them to run long. It meant money out of Tommy's pocket. They dismissed us and told us to seriously think about what Tommy had said. To be responsible members of McKipson's. And to remember the future of McKipson's was in our hands.

I walked to my car feeling dirty and cheap. Like a phony. I wanted to punch myself. No, I wanted to punch Tommy McKipson, and everyone else with their boot on the neck of the working man. Not only did this bastard want us to give him the best years of our lives, now he expected us to give the money he paid us right back to him. It sounded a little too much like share cropping to me. I thought Abraham Lincoln had freed the slaves. I guess not. It was like everything else they taught you in school –a lie.

I drove home that night with a heavy heart. Somewhere someone was laughing. But it wasn't me.

Chapter 15
(late November)

Before I knew it, it was time for Thanksgiving: cranberry sauce, stuffing, pumpkin pie, and turkey. I never cared much for holidays. I always found them stressful or lonely. I could understand why the suicide rate always spiked around the winter solstice. I think it could all be equated to either too much family and booze, or not enough, or a combination of those things.

I had the day off from work, and since Roo was still in Florida, I decided to spend the day at my parents' house. It was nothing spectacular, just my parents, siblings, and my degenerate ass sitting around the dining room table. Holidays at my boy-hood home were always uneventful. My family was pretty squeaky clean (with the exception of me). We watched the parade, ate turkey, and napped as college football played in the background. Afterwards I went over to Rainy's house and met her mom, Linda, for the first time. That's when things really got interesting.

Rainy (an only child) had been raised by her mother (a devote follower of the treat your children as friends philosophy), and as a result Rainy told Linda everything, much to my chagrin. They were more like sisters than mother and daughter. And although Linda liked to view herself as more of a mentor, than a mother, she still liked to spoil Rainy unconditionally and give her anything her little heart desired.

Her house looked like a shrine to Rainy. It was filled with all of Rainy's trophies, awards, and ribbons from various pageants and contests she had been in over the years. Linda had been entering her in these things ever since she was a kid. And thanks to Linda, Rainy appeared to be Tucson's answer to Jon Benet Ramsey. I had never seen so many pictures of one person. It was like a tiny museum. Obviously Linda was living vicariously through Rainy. It was a little scary.

Couple this with the fact that Rainy's father had taken off when she was two years old, to start a new family with his mistress in Oregon, and it was easy to see why Rainy was so tightly packed with issues (she suffered from severe mood swings, constantly had to be the center of attention, and harbored fantasies of moving to New York and becoming a movie star; which I never understood seeing how Hollywood is where people go to become movie stars, perhaps she had theater and movie star mixed up, I don't know).

I showed up to Rainy's house high and twenty minutes late. It was just us, Linda, and Rainy's grandparents (a couple of mummies from a retirement community in Green Valley). So, I didn't see any reason to show up early. I figured it would be a pretty lax event. As usual, I was wrong.

Rainy's mom answered the door and invited me in. She looked like an old, tired, version of Rainy. You could tell there was a time when she had broken a few hearts, but those days were long gone. Men and life had given her a pretty good ass whopping. Don't get me wrong though, given half the chance, I'd still fuck her. She had a nice body and dressed very sharp and stylish for her age. She looked kinda like a news anchor.

"Vincente?" she asked inviting me in.

"Yes, sorry I'm late. Dinner ran long at my parents. You know how that is. It's a pleasure to finally meet you, though, you have a lovely house," I said in my most charming voice.

"Likewise, I'm sure," she said.

I placed one foot over the threshold and continued with my spiel.

"You know, modern theorists have found a direct correlation between a home's *feng shui* and the owner's intelligence. And I'm getting a strong sense of chi coming from…"

She cut me off.

"Cut the bullshit, Mr. Vasquez,, and please come in. I'd offer to show you around, but Rainy has informed me that you come over quite regularly."

I was surprised at Linda's dryness. Her pedantic tone was a stark contrast to Rainy's bubbly personality. I figured it must suit her well in her job as an English teacher at the women's prison.

"Yeah, we hang out sometimes in the morning," I said.

"Yes, I'm perfectly aware of these morning make-out sessions."

I almost swallowed my gum. She caught me off guard with that one. Thankfully Rainy walked in and saved me.

"You're here," she said throwing her arms around me. "Come meet my grandparents."

We walked into the dining room and were greeted by two of the oldest people I had ever seen. Grandma and grandpa had to be in their early hundreds. They looked like they needed to be embalmed. They were already at the dinner table, plates in front of them, prepared to eat. Apparently, I was holding up the show. Rainy introduced me to the old lady.

"Grandma, this is Vincente."

I extended my hand. The old lady looked at it funnily before grabbing it.

"Have you excepted Jesus as your personal lord and savior, Vincente?" she asked.

It turned out the old lady was a bible beating Jesus fanatic.

"Knock it off, grandma," Rainy snapped before I could answer. "And this is my opa," she said introducing me to the oldman.

He extended his hand and I grasped it firmly. "Nice to meet you sir, " I said. His hand felt brittle and lifeless. I eased my grip worried that I might break him. He barely seemed alive.

"Have a seat," Rainy's mom said. "I was just getting ready to serve dinner. We like to be very *punctual* around here."

I couldn't tell if that was a slight against me or not, but I assumed it was. I sat down and a plate was placed in front of me. The food looked sub-standard and bland, but I put it away and complimented Linda on her prowess in the kitchen.

"Thank you, Vincente, you're always quick with a compliment aren't you? No wonder Rainy finds you so intriguing."

All through dinner, Linda kept trying to glare at me nonchalantly, out of the corner of her eye. She was obviously trying to size me up. It was beginning to make me uncomfortable. Rainy, oblivious to the situation, made a sculpture with her mashed potatoes. And grandma just went on, and on, about God (it was worse than mass). The oldman, for his part, just shoveled spoonful, after spoonful, of peas smothered in honey into his mouth. It was all very strange to me. Were holidays always like this at the Rusch house? It made me long for my family and our boring dinners.

Grandma continued to ramble.

"Just yesterday, in his sermon, brother Thomas was expressing the importance of abstinence amongst our youth. And I couldn't agree more. What are your views on the subject Vincente?"

Linda interjected before I could answer.

"Mother, please. Abstinence is an antiquated notion, heaped upon us by men afraid of female sexuality and freedom. I prefer my daughter engage in responsible sexual acts and learn from her mistakes, no matter *how big* they might be, than practice abstinence."

"Hear, hear," I said emphatically.

"So, Vincente, Rainy tells me you have a girlfriend," Linda said staring at me.

"Well, no, I mean, I did, but we broke up. It was when me and Rainy first met, but we broke up. I'm single now. I don't have a girlfriend currently, because we broke up. I'm single," I fumbled.

"Really. Well, that's quite interesting," Linda said doubtingly. "Rainy also told me you're a marijuana addict."

Grandma looked on in horror. Grandpa continued to fumble with his peas. Rainy just gave me a silly little smile, as if she had done nothing wrong in divulging all my dirty laundry to her mother.

I laughed nervously, "Addict is a strong word, mam. I mean, I partake occasionally, but only to relax, never to the point of senselessness."

"That's funny, I was under the impression that you got, how did Rainy put it…baked daily."

I wanted to melt into my chair and disappear. It was like the Spanish inquisition. At the end of dinner Linda asked if I would care for coffee and dessert. I said I would.

"How do you like your coffee?" Linda asked.

For some reason I just couldn't say black. I had to try and be a comedian. It wasn't even a conscious effort. It was just years of being a smartass working in autopilot. This innate fire that burned inside me. As the words left my mouth I could already feel the shame in what I had said. It was like watching it on TV, it wasn't me speaking, but somebody else. I wanted to stop mid-sentence, knowing full well this wasn't the time or place, but the words were already leaving my mouth. It was out of my hands.

"Like my women," I said. "Strong and black!"

Grandma seemed disgusted by my sense of humor. Linda nodded her head in disapproval, and Rainy just stared at the floor embarrassed. A silence fell across the room. And for the first time that night the oldman said something. He laughed.

Chapter 16
(late, late November)

When Roo got back from Florida, after Thanksgiving, she had changed. She wasn't the happy go lucky person she had been. She now drank periodically throughout the day and was more prone to bouts of sullenness. Not only that, but to compound the problem, she had taken up the habit of swallowing vicodin when she drank. She'd get real loopy and I'd worry she might stop breathing in the middle of the night. The last thing I wanted to do was wake up next to a dead girl.

She also started carrying around her dead sister's purse everywhere she went (an old green army bag purchased at a thrift store somewhere). It was the saddest purse I had ever seen. It would lay on the floor, staring up at me sometimes, longing for it's now deceased owner. But despite the purse's gloomy appearance Roo took it everywhere. It was like her adopted child, an orphan. I could tell she was afloat a sea of melancholy, but what could I do? I, myself, was changing.

Our relationship no longer contented me. I was merely going through the motions. Rainy consumed my thoughts now. Ever since that night at the Halloween party I couldn't get her out of my mind. I wanted to call it off with Roo, but in her current state I was worried how it might affect her. So, instead I stuck it out, a trooper. All the while growing resentful towards her, the purse, and my current state. And never sensing the bomb that await me.

Chapter 17
(very early December)

It's funny how fast things can change. In the blink of an eye you could be dead. Or win the lottery. Or have the girl you love rip your heart out through your ass. It's a thin line between love and hate, and the human heart is a fickle creature. But there I go again, getting ahead of myself.

The more I got to know Rainy the less I liked her. I had come to the conclusion that she was the ultimate oxymoron, she was both a cock-tease and a whore (if that's even possible). Her gold patina was quickly starting to fade. Cracks were beginning to show in the façade. It was like I had peeked behind the curtain, and found out the Wizard of Oz was nothing but a crusty old white dude. The magic was gone.

I decided the best thing I could do was pretend she didn't exist anymore. I was tired of chasing her around like a lost puppy, while she played with my emotions. Allow me to elaborate.

The melon that broke the monkey's back came the first week in December. One of the flunkies in the meat department had decided to throw an especially early Christmas party. And seeing how I have a natural distaste for parties, and Roo was now back in town, and I was pretty secure in the direction me and Rainy's relationship was heading, I had no interest in attending. I figured the whole thing would be rather uneventful anyway, but numerous coworkers were sure to inform me otherwise. The first was Dominic Greene, one of the night cashiers.

"Yo, where were you last night? Your girl was doin' you wrong, man."

It was now common knowledge around work that I had a serious thing for Rainy, and that we were hanging out on a regular basis.

"What are you talking about?" I asked.

"Miss Thang! She was gonna fuck Brad in the bathroom last night!"

Surely he was joking. There was no way that could have happened.

"Brad, from produce? Yeah, right," I answered.

"Fo real man. I guess he had her pants down and everything. He was getting ready to stick that shit in till Greg got wind of what was going on and broke it up. I guess he doesn't like people fucking in his bathroom."

My stomach spasmed. I could feel my intestines writhing like worms. I wanted to puke. It was like being shot. A part of me didn't want to believe it, but somehow I knew it had to be true. Dominic wasn't one to make shit up. I composed myself as best I could.

"Well, good for him," I said trying to act indifferent. "I guess he gots more game than me."

"Man, don't try an' play it so cool. I know you wanted to be the first one to crack that clam."

He was right. I had. I took it as a direct threat on my masculinity. Brad was 120 pound weakling. Rainy was at least five inches taller than him. If he was able to succeed where I had failed, what did that say about me? I must be lower than low –scum. A mutant unworthy of love. I had licked this chick's snatch like an ice-cream cone and this was my thanks! How could she, that little bitch! I felt like a fool. A jackass. I didn't want to believe she could do me that dirty, but when other people started telling me the same thing, I had no choice but to accept the truth.

When Rainy got to work that day, I walked up fuming, and confronted her.

"You're a whore," I told her with heartless eyes.

"What," she said, as if she hadn't heard me.

"You heard me, you're a whore!"

She looked at me confused.

"That's right, I heard about you and Brad in the bathroom you fuckin' skank! What the fuck was that all about?"

She stayed quiet with a puzzled look on her face. I could hear the wheels turning in her head. Then, unexpectedly, she exploded like Vesuvius.

"FUCK YOU, VINNIE!" she said.

Her anger startled me. After all, I was the victim here.

"I was drunk, you have a girlfriend, and were not together!"

I didn't know what to say. She was right, but it didn't stop my heart from hurting.

"Yeah, don't think I forgot that you're with somebody!" she continued. "I'm not stupid. I know you like to think you're smarter than everyone, but you're not. I know you didn't break up with your girlfriend. So what does that make you, Vinnie? I guess you're a whore too!"

"What are you talking about? I broke up with my girlfriend weeks ago," I feebly lied.

"Really? Then how come you never call me at night? How come I only see you in the morning before school? I'm not stupid."

Not knowing what to say, I walked away disgusted. It was one thing to almost fuck another guy, but how dare she question my intelligence! That's where I drew the line.

I walked back into the deli and helped the next customer in line. As far as I was concerned, me and Rainy were through. I made sure to avoid her the rest of the day.

Chapter 18
(December)

I went home that night in a foul mood. I was supposed to go over to Roo's, but I didn't feel like being around anyone, especially Roo. I kept imaging Rainy in the bathroom with Brad. His enormous cock (that undoubtedly dwarfed mine in comparison) ready to harpoon Rainy, as she lay on the bathroom sink, legs spread, pussy wet with anticipation. Over and over again the scene played out in my mind. I couldn't get it out of my head.

I rolled a joint in hope that weed might calm my mind. It didn't work. The image was still there. I saw her, clear as day, bent over the sink, as Brad prepared to enter her from behind –her legs quivering in ecstasy. It was maddening. Over, and over, and over, again.

I needed a distraction. Out of pure frustration, I took a long deep drag on the joint till the cherry glowed like the Devil's dick. Then as I choked and coughed on the acrid smoke, I buried the joint into my forearm, extinguishing it's life. The cherry bit into my flesh creating a sharp pain. I could smell the flesh burning as I held the joint tight against my arm. It felt comforting. It's what I felt I deserved. But it wasn't enough. I was a sewer rat. A fool. I was every manner of lowly creature. I needed to redeem myself. I needed to hurt something, like I myself was being hurt –that something was Roo.

I called her up and told her it was over, plain and simple. That I wasn't into her. She started to cry and say she didn't understand. She begged me to think it over. I said, "no doing". I was done. I had found someone new. When she asked me who it was, I said it didn't matter and hung up the phone. I sat on the couch thinking about what I had just done. I felt even worse than before. What kind of person was I? I felt like crying. So I did.

Chapter 19
(December)

I don't know why I had such a disregard for girls feelings. I guess I would have to blame it on June, she was the first girl to really hurt me. *Ahh*, June, clad in Doc Martens and a floral-print dress –my first true love. No one hurts you like that. I read somewhere once, that the magical thing about first love is, you think it will never end. I know I did. I thought for sure June was the girl I was going to marry. We started dating my junior year of high school. She was a sophomore.

In my opinion, sophomore girls are always the best. They're more open to suggestion and experimentation. They're eager to please and belong. Freshman girls are just silly and immature. They're still in that junior high state of mind. And senior chicks are consumed with what they are going to do after graduation and fucking college guys. While junior girls are neurotic balls of hormones trapped somewhere between being a girl and a woman. I guess you could say high school girls are like bananas, you don't go to the store and buy the ripe ones, you pick the ones that are still a little green.

Me and June dated all through high school and when she turned twenty (and I twenty-one) we got our own place and moved in together. It lasted six months before she broke up with me. Sure, maybe I was constantly going out without her. And maybe I didn't help keep our place clean, or treat her as good as she deserved, or even tell her I loved her, or one of the other million things girls need to feel secure, but I truly felt invested. I had given her my heart. I thought love knew no bounds. What a crock!

I would have to say the final straw was New Year's Eve. It was supposed to be our first together in our new place. We were going to make a night of it, just the two of us. June went out and procured two live lobsters, steaks, and a bottle of nice champagne (which she had to have a co-worker buy for her on the account she was still under age). I'll admit, maybe I didn't make the wisest of decisions, but I had just turned twenty-one and was new to the whole bar scene. So when one of the guys from work asked if I wanted to go out for a pre-celebratory drink, I couldn't resist.

We ended up at a strip club where we stayed till 10 o'clock when it closed. I got home to June's blood shot eyes well before midnight, but the night was already ruined. The food was cold and I ended up passing out in a drunken stupor before 11 o'clock. Two days later she moved out.

After June left I spiraled into a deep depression. I started spending most of my time, heavily drinking and what I like to call "hogging"(a.k.a picking up fat drunk girls at the bars for the sole purpose of fucking and chucking). I had come to learn that keeping the company of fat chicks was easier, they didn't expect much and you could treat them however you wanted. They were easy targets. In our society, at least for girls, there is nothing more important than being pretty. So when girls aren't, they usually have low self-esteem and are readily available for all kinds of abuse. I know it sounds cruel, but it was a means of protecting myself. This way there would be no emotions involved. I refused to let myself get hurt again.

Things went on like this for over a year. My breaking point didn't come till sometime later. I woke up in bed, hot, sweaty and with a raging hangover. It was the middle of summer and hotter than Hades. The air conditioning had stopped working sometime during the night, and a single fly was buzzing around the room, occasionally landing on a random pile of dirty laundry. I rolled over, in an attempt to cool off, and was greeted by a perspiring behemoth of a woman. I had no memory of bringing her home, but yet there she was. She smelled of tobacco and beer, and sweat rolled off her pimply back as she snored like a grizzly. I leaned over the bed and wretched into the waste basket. I had hit rock bottom.

After that, I had a moment of clarity, I quit drinking and stuck strictly to smoking weed. I also made the attempt to start socializing more. I started hanging out with my cousin Mona on a regular basis, and eventually got in touch with Carlos and started hanging around with his crew of friends. But without my liquid courage I was forced into a life of celibacy for the next eight months (sans liquor I didn't have the nerve to approach girls), it's then that I met Roo and slowly started drinking again. The rest you know.

In hindsight, breaking up with Roo was probably the best thing I could have done (for her at least). It had become a relationship of convenience. Sure, maybe I hadn't done it in the most tactful way, but it was for the best. She was growing more attached everyday and I wasn't. I had built a wall around myself to keep from getting too attached to Roo. This way I wouldn't miss her when she was gone. I knew what we had wasn't going to last forever (nothing does). She was merely a stepping stone to re-launch my love life. A diving board, if you will, launching me in to the dating pool. I know it's fucked up sounding, but people do it all the time. Life can be a scary place. Sometimes people will do the most despicable things, just to keep from having to wade through all the shit alone.

But the funny thing was, despite all the walls I had put up and everything I had told myself, I did miss Roo. I missed the sweet smell of her breath in the morning. The way she'd roll her eyes when she got embarrassed. And a hundred other little things I will probably never understand.

Chapter 20
(December)

Needless to say, after my little stunt with Roo, I was out of the crew. It all happened quite easy. I wasn't a vested member. I had been accepted because I was an old friend of Carlos and Roo's boyfriend. Now I was viewed as the guy who had fucked over Roo as she was mourning the death of her sister. Even Carlos disowned me (under Leah's orders) –that fucking sellout! We had been friends for years and he turned his back on me like it was nothing, and all for a pretentious piece of ass named Leah (it was alright though, karma got even with him, when to his embarrassment a year later, Leah left him for the latest of her new causes –a woman).

The only people I was still cool with were Santos and Emma. After all, they had been my friends before all this Roo nonsense. They'd still come over to my house, on occasion, to hang-out and get high. But other than that I was alone and suffering from a serious friend deficit.

There is a lot of down time when you are single. It can be quite lonely. I tried to spend as much time as I could away from home. I'd hang out in bookstores, reading, sipping black coffee, and trying to look intelligent. Hoping I might meet some girl. I never did though.

I'd go to the movies and watch independent films. Kick around the mall. Anything to keep from having to stare at the same four walls of my apartment. It was maddening.

Every night after work I would go home, watch cartoons, and get high till 3 in the morning. Then I'd get up the next day at 11am, smoke a bowl, watch TV for a couple of hours, eat some sugar frosted kid's cereal, and take a nap till 2pm when I had to get ready for work (which had taken on a new dimension of stress as well).

I had never been in the position of having to see a former love interest almost daily. Then again, I had never been romantically involved with a co-worker. It was like having a wound constantly reopened. It made my stomach turn. I would never be able to get over Rainy as long as I had to see her all the time. And trust me, I hated her guts with every fiber of my being, but at the same time I was still inexplicably attracted to her. In the words of Humbert Humbert, "The poison was in the wound, you see. And the wound wouldn't heal." Life went on like this for days, with no end in sight. And there she was, a constant reminder of my ineptitude. A testament to my failure. It was a dark time. I slowly started to unravel again.

The thing about depression is it creeps in like a fog, quietly and slowly. You barely notice it at first, and by the time you do it is too late. You're engulfed, unable to even see the hand in front of your face.

I hadn't cleaned the cat box in over a week and I had piles of laundry everywhere. The sink was overrun with dishes, and a trail of tiny ants had taken up residence in my kitchen. I had been getting by washing the occasional shirt or pair of pants in the bathroom sink, but eventually I ran out of clothes and was forced to do laundry. Everything I owned was dirty. I started gathering things up and sorting them by colors. I picked up a pair a pants I hadn't worn or washed in months. I could feel something in the pocket. It felt like money. I plunged my hand in hoping to find a twenty and pulled out a tiny piece of crumpled paper instead. It had a number and a name on it, Trish. It was the number of that sweaty, pimply-backed, grizzly I had nailed months ago before I had hooked up with Roo. A tiny ember lit inside my brain. I could feel the hum of my libido. I decided I was going to call this girl. I was tired of masturbating to scrambled porn on the pay-pay-per-view network. I needed something to break up the monotony. I knew this would be an easy conquest and call for least amount of work on my part. So, I picked up the phone and made the call.

"Hi, is this Trish?"

"Yeah," a voice answered back.

"Hey, this is Vincente, we met a few months ago, I had been wanting to call you but lost your number, then I was going through an old pair of pants today and found it, what's going on?"

I suddenly felt like a fool for calling. Had I no shame? Was there anything I wouldn't do for a piece of ass?

"Vincente???"

"Yeah, tall guy, we met at Gotham then you came back to my place and chilled out."

There was silence on the other line. She was trying to recall me. A tiny voice inside me said, hang up.

"Vincent with the green eyes?" she asked.

"Yeah, that's me!" I said like a fool.

"Hey, how have you been…that was awhile ago."

"I know, like I said, I had been wanting to call you but couldn't find your number. So, what have you been up to?"

I was praying she didn't have a boyfriend, even though I severely doubted it.

"Nothing just hanging out."

"Oh yeah, have you gone to Gotham since then?"

I hated making this sort of small talk. It was painfully awkward. The pretenses we humans have. Animals don't have to do this. They just walk behind a bush and fuck. Is this what we had crawled out of the primordial ooze for? For mindless chit-chat before meaningless sex? *Uggghhh*, if that was the case, you could keep your evolution.

"Actually, no," she said. "I was sooooo drunk that night."

"Me too. So, we should get together some time. Hang out," I said trying to get to the point and be nonchalant at the same time.

"That would be cool."

"Well, what are you doing tonight?" I ventured.

And that was it. The trap was set.

Chapter 21
(December)

When Trish showed up at my place I hadn't even bothered to put anything decent on. I answered the door in a pair of dirty jeans and an old t-shirt. I wasn't worried about impressing her. She could take it or leave it, as far as I was concerned. I was surprised when I opened the door though, she wasn't as bad looking as I remembered. I mean, she wasn't gonna win any beauty competitions any time soon, but she wasn't a complete beast. Of course she was large, I mean, very large, but she had the face of a cherub and one of the prettiest smiles I had ever seen. I ignored the fact that she had a second smaller stomach hanging over her pussy and invited her in.

I had been drinking since I got off the phone with Trish, so I had a pretty good buzz going. She sat down on the couch and I offered her a beer, as we made more small talk.

"Were you able to find my place pretty easily?" I asked.

"Yeah, for the most part."

I looked her up and down, discreetly, as she sat there. She had big floppy tits, but they didn't look half bad when they were supported by that enormous bra she wore. They kept peeking out of the top of her low cut shirt, like two fleshy bowling balls. And her legs, sticking out of the bottom of her short skirt, looked pretty nice as well –thick and muscular (they had to be to carry that load). Not to sound like a fattist (as long as a girl has a thick hour glass shape, she is fair game in my book, no matter how much she weighs), it's just that some girls diamond's are buried a little deeper in the rough than others.

But the truth of the matter is, I felt totally at ease around Trish. I wasn't nervous at all. I felt like I could be myself. It was nice. We sat and drank beer and bullshitted for a couple of hours before I made my move.

After I was borderline drunk, I asked her if she wanted to take a tour of my apartment (this was my typical move, once things had progressed this far, it worked 90% of the time). She said of course, surely anticipating (and probably desiring) my nefarious motives, as I showed her around my palatial one bedroom home.

When we came to the final stop on our tour –the bedroom; I left the light off, so it was only dimly lit by the hall light, causing a romantic tone. It was all very suave, on my part.

"And this is the bedroom," I said with a flourish of my hands.

She looked around.

"Nice," she said.

"Here," I said. "sit on my bed. Look at how comfortable it is."

She sat on the edge of my bed shyly. I sat next to her and put my hand on her thigh.

"Nice, huh?" I asked.

"Yeah," she said.

I leaned in and started kissing her as I slid my hand between her legs, forcing my way between her chubby thighs. By the time my hand found it's destination she was already wet. I could feel it through her panties. I slid them to the side and slipped two of my fingers inside her. She laid back on the bed, moaned, and started struggling to undo my pants, but she was all thumbs. I helped her by unbuckling my belt and undoing my fly. She plunged her hand into my boxers and started squeezing and yanking at my dick. I don't know whether it was from the excitement, or if this was her natural technique, but either way she was too rough. I overlooked this little technicality though and really started getting into it. Pre-cum dripped from the tip of my dick. I was beyond horny. I unbuttoned the first few buttons on her blouse and put one of her flabby breasts in my mouth.

What a mistake.

My tongue was poked by a short, stray, nipple hair she had forgot to pluck. But I could tell she was starting to get into it, as well. She kept wiggling her hips like a fish and thrusting her pelvis, pushing my fingers deeper into her.

"I want you inside me," she said in a hot heavy whisper.

I had to think quick. Even though I was drunk and horny, I wasn't trying to mount this piggy. I had already made that error once before. This time I had something else in mind.

"I have a stomachache," I whispered back. " I drank too much. How about you give me head instead?"

I wasn't sure she would go for it. For a split second, I thought I might have shot myself in the foot. It started to look like it was gonna be another night of jacking-off for me. But to my surprise, she took the bait.

She went down on me. And she did it good. I mean real good. I don't know, there is just something about big girls, they always try harder. At any rate, after that it became a weekly routine. She'd come over, we'd make out a little bit, then she would give me head. Occasionally, if I could tell she wasn't in to it, I'd finger her a little bit to get her in the mood, but that was the extent of it. We never had sex. I figured maybe she wouldn't get too attached that way and I could save her some eventual heart ache –after all, I wasn't trying to hurt this girl. Plus I had no interest in having sex with her in the first place, I wasn't attracted to her. I realize how cruel it must sound, but I like to think we were using each other. I mean, Trish had to be getting something out of this. I don't know. Maybe I'm being naïve.

If I wasn't such a shallow piece of shit. I probably could have been in a very happy relationship with Trish. She was a cool chick. She actually had a personality. All too often, hot chicks are nothing but, vacuous empty husks caked in mascara. Plus Trish was a grade-A cock sucker, a rare talent indeed. But in the words of Popeye the Sailor, I am what I am, and there was nothing I could do about it. Sometimes all you can do is play the cards your dealt.

Chapter 22
(very late December)

Christmas had come and gone without a hitch, and here we were standing at the dawn of a new millennium. Everything was changing. Nothing was certain. It was the end of an era and people were scared shitless. We were all wading through a sea of "pre-millennium tension". Who knew what might happen next. The world might end.

It seemed as high-tech as computers had become they couldn't handle a simple thing like a two digit rollover from xx99 to xx00. Apparently this completely fucked them up, and threatened to bring our highly dependant-on-computer world, to a screeching halt.

First the banks would fail and social order would break down. There'd be riots and food shortages, plagues, and famine. Rivers would run backwards and toads and locusts would rain from the sky. The earth would become a scorched wasteland ruled by leather clad neo-punks, and their chopped up muscle cars. Eventually the seas would run red with blood, and the earth would open up and demons would pour out. In short, it would be an apocalyptic nightmare that would have people praying for the rapture.

And, as is human nature, we had to give title to this inevitable armageddon. An event of this magnitude, begged to be named. But what would the worlds thinkers, poets, and scholars call this time of uncertainty? What words carried the weight and somberness to describe this impending doom? After much deliberation amongst society's logicians, there was only one conceivable answer:

Y2K

That was it, Y2K. That was the best they could give us.

What a joke!

It sound like something cooked up in a think tank by a bunch of first year ad executives. It was pure bullshit. This wasn't the name for what the world at large was feeling. This sounded like a new line of Nike sneakers. I saw it as further proof of the decline of western civilization. But what did I know?

My cousin Mona was throwing a New Year's Eve party, and since I didn't have anyone to spend the evening with, I decided, against my better judgment, to attend. Besides, I figured if the world was gonna end, I might as well be around a few other people; hell, I might even get lucky.

Mona had just moved in with her putz of a boyfriend (David) and his playboy best friend, Chad. We had met the two of them one Friday night while out at The Wildcat House. The Cat House, as regulars lovingly referred to it, was completely different world from the bohemian hot-spots that I frequented downtown while dating Roo. It was as straight up meat-market. Everyone there was dying to get laid. The place reeked of roofies and desperation. If you couldn't score here, you were either me, or a complete loser. But for some reason my cousin loved the place. So there we were.

It was a night like any other. We stood at the edge of the dance floor, drinking long island ice-tea's from a 34 ounce carafe (these were the house specialty, made with enough liquor to peel paint), and watching people dance.

After my second carafe of booze I was struck with the uncontrollable urge to piss. Which is always a bummer whenever you are trying to catch a buzz; the last thing you wanna do is break your seal, but when nature calls what choice do you have. So, I turn my back for like two seconds, and when I get back some schmuck is all over my cousin like a wet blanket. Where this clown even got the nerve to approach her I will never know. She was way out of his league. I figured it was only a matter of milliseconds before Mona dispatched this fool, but the next thing I know, she's out on the floor cuttin' a rug with this kid. I guess she could see something in him, because before you knew it they were dating, and couple of months later, they were shacking up together. So, what the fuck do I know?

After Mona started dating David we didn't hang out as much. And when we did, it seemed like David and his corn-buddy Chad always had to tag along. Chad was a world-class slime ball. He made me sick. He was tall, and tan, with blue eyes and blond hair, and all the ladies seemed to love him. Every time we went somewhere he had to make it a point to flirt with the waitress and get her number. I was certain he was only doing it to rub my nose in it. Mona was well aware of my female troubles, and I figured it was only natural for her to tell her boyfriend (that's what couples do, they share shit), so I was pretty sure when David was alone with his other girlfriend (Chad), he was telling him all of my business. It pissed me off. It was none of his concern, what was going on in my personal life.

Understandably, I made it quite public I didn't care for Chad, in my own passive aggressive way. When ever he was around I tended to be more reticent and give him the cold shoulder. He had to notice. Or maybe he didn't. He was rather dense. Actually, he was dumber than hammered shit. I don't know what ladies saw in him, but some way or another, he always managed to be juggling at least three.

At any rate, here I was at a New Year's Eve party where I knew next to no one, trying desperately to fit in. My cousin, Mona, informed me that two of Chad's girls were in attendance that evening. One of them seemed completely oblivious to the fact, while the other one was obviously distraught. Chad, on the other hand, appeared to be unmoved by this predicament. He sauntered around, like cock of the walk, bragging to his buddies that two of his "bitches" happened to be there. Apparently, in all his infinite wisdom, he had forgotten that he invited both of them. That or he was such a scum-bag he didn't even have the tact to pretend like he cared about these females.

At any rate, I stood back against the wall, beer in hand, watching the proceedings. I didn't feel like talking to anyone but Mona, but she was busy entertaining her friends from work, so I didn't want to be a pest. Instead I focused my attention on Chad's girlfriend, the distraught one.

The later it got, the more upset she appeared. She was pacing back and forth, drinking heavily, and chain smoking. I didn't understand why she just didn't leave. Why was she putting herself through this torture? When I saw her walk outside I decided to follow. I wanted to talk to her. Perhaps I could *comfort* her. I found her outside crying into her hands.

"Hey," I said. "are you alright?"

She looked up at me. Her mascara was running. She wasn't a bad looking girl. Not really my style, kind of cheap looking, but she was cute. Too cute for Chad.

"Yeah, I'm okay," she said. "my boyfriend is just a dick. That's all."

"You're talking about, Chad right?"

"Yeah, are you a friend of his?"

"No. Chad's no friend of mine. I'm Mona's cousin, Vincente," I said extending my hand.

"Nice to meet you," she said sniffling and trying to compose herself. "You're cousin is really cool. She is funny. I like her."

"Yeah, she's a nice chick." I reached in my pocket and pulled out a pack of Camel Lights. "Here, you wanna smoke?" I asked.

"Yeah, thanks."

"I know it's none of my business, but why are you hanging out here? I know Chad invited another girl. You don't deserve this shit."

"I know. I just really like him. He is just so awesome and smart."

Were we talking about the same guy here? Chad was neither of these things.

"Him?! I know tons of guys better than him!"

She started to cry again. Maybe she was thinking about Chad's awesomeness. I walked over and hugged her.

"Come on, you don't need to cry over this guy," I said consoling her.

She hugged me back and looked up at me with big, tear-filled, puppy dog eyes. I could fill my libido rising from it's slumber (something about crying chicks always turns me on). This was it. I was gonna make my move. I leaned in to kiss her. Puckering my lips.

She turned her head, rejecting my advances, and stepped away from me. My lips careened through the air, missing their mark.

"Thanks, for talking to me," she said making her escape. "I'm gonna go back inside now."

I could feel myself filling with chagrin. I wanted to go somewhere and hide. Talk about a loser! Why was I so fucking awkward?

"No, problem," I said turning around and walking away.

I didn't understand it. What was wrong with me? Here I was standing on the cusp of a new millennium and I was still striking out. I walked back inside my cousins apartment and looked around. I still didn't know anyone there. They were all strange faces. I had never felt so alone. A strange guy walked over. He was a little tipsy.

"Hey man, what do you think is gonna happen at midnight?" he asked.

"Hopefully armageddon," I answered dryly.

He gave me an odd look and walked away. I walked over to the kitchen, grabbed a bottle of whiskey off the counter, and took a few hard swallows. I felt like everyone was staring at me. Like they were gossiping about what had just transpired outside.

Can you believe it! He tried to kiss that girl outside. He's a strange one, sir. Did I ever tell you about the time he put a lit joint out on his arm? He should see a shrink! Chases high school girls? Unbelievable! He went down on her for how long? Then she was going to screw someone else in a bathroom! Shameful. It's his own fault, that one. He has problems. I'm telling you he's crazy! He hardly has any friends, sir. I think he should be committed.

I grabbed a couple of beers for the road. Then I got in my car and left without saying goodbye to anyone. If the world was going to end I wanted to be alone, I decided. Maybe I'd watch Dick Clark. I was sure, by this time, they had pulled him out of his sarcophagus, dusted him off, and stuck him in front of a live television camera. At least there was still some things you could depend on.

By the time I got home, I was dog tired and slightly drunk. The whiskey had had a chance to take an effect on the ride home. I fell asleep on the couch without even seeing the ball drop. I woke up the next morning and felt a cramp in my stomach. I had to take a hot whiskey shit. I sat on the toilet and did my business. When I finished

I flushed it all away. Since the toilet still worked, I figured the world hadn't come to an end the night before. It was all a lot of hype. Scaremongering perpetrated by a, brain-dead, mass media. Talk about anti-climatic. What a let down. I brushed my teeth and put my clothes on for work. I guessed I'd have to wait a little longer to see that place burn.

Chapter 23
(mid January)

Sure, it was a new year and a new millennium, but it was still the same old shit. Work sucked, my love life was in the toilet, and at times I felt like I didn't have a friend in the world. I started to wonder, if I died, how long it would take for people to realize. Like, if I was to go peacefully in my sleep, or something.

A week? Two weeks maybe?

I figured after that I would start to stink the place up and someone would call the police. They'd have to kick in my door, and have the little old lady who lived up stairs identify my body.

"Yes, that's him officer. The wanna-be player."

It wasn't a comforting thought.

To distract myself from these morbid notions I started reading Dicken's *Great Expectations*. I enjoyed the somber tone of the book. I felt I could relate to Pip's eternal longing. I too, knew what it was like to be at the mercy of the wealthy, and long for a coldhearted woman. Ol' Chuck was a true word-smith, mixing humor, social commentary, poetry and sentimentality. I found solace in his words.

Then of course the inevitable happened.

One night, out of the blue, Trish called me drunk and crying. She asked why I had never asked her to be my girlfriend. I was a little surprised. We had only been hanging out for a little over a month, and I didn't think she would get attached so fast. Not to mention the fact, that we had never gone on anything even remotely resembling a date.

But the jig was up. She wanted to take things to the next level. Everything inside of me said to lie to her. To tell her that I just wanted to take things slow. After all, I didn't want to lose her and her wonderful BJs. But I couldn't do it. I had to tell her the truth, that I wasn't into her. I refused to lie and string her along. My conscience wouldn't let me do it.

When I told her how I felt she cussed me out and called me a jerk. She said I had been using her. She even went as far as to tell me I had a little dick. I didn't let it get to me though. I knew it was just the anger talking. I hung up the phone and thought about what I had done. I didn't feel too good about it, but what was done, was done. And yet another chapter closed in the love life of Vincente Vasquez.

Chapter 24
(February)

It was a few days before Valentine's day and I was feeling as alone as ever. I was starting to wish I had lied to Trish. At least then I wouldn't have to spend the night alone. I mulled around work in a borderline catatonic state. While slicing roast beef I would suddenly imagine pressing my wrist into the spinning blade of the slicer. I would fall to the ground and die a slow tragic death. Before the burial they'd hold a viewing at the store. I'd be placed in the deli's cold case amongst the ambrosia and potato salad –a tomato rosette resting in my lapel. June, Roo, and Trish would come to stand over me and gloat at my demise. These strange fantasies became more frequent and elaborate as time went on, and then the strangest thing happened. After having ignored each other for the last two months Rainy came up and talked to me.

"How you doing?" she asked.

I got a knot in my stomach. I hadn't been expecting this. It made me nervous. I suddenly found myself licking my lips and wondering if I looked alright.

"I'm doing good," I said. "How about you?"

"I'm good. Have you found yourself a Valentine yet? Its just around the corner," she said coyly.

"I have a couple of prospects," I lied.

Then she hit me with a bomb.

"I've missed you, you jerk!"

"Jerk?! What did I do?" I asked genuinely shocked.

"Getting mad over that whole Brad thing," she said rolling her eyes.

"You were gonna fuck some guy in a bathroom. I think that warrants me getting upset."

"I don't even like Brad. I was drunk. It was stupid of me. It's not a big deal," she said casually.

"Whatever," I said annoyed. The old wound starting to ache.

From the look on her face I could tell she was getting frustrated. I guess she had just been expecting me to take her back with open arms.

"Forget it! I thought maybe you were ready to grow up, but I guess not!" she said in a bitchy tone.

That bitchy anger was always lying just beneath her pretty exterior, waiting to rear it's ugly head and show her true colors. I got worried I might chase her off (although I was still mad at her, I was elated that she was even talking to me). I changed my tune. Bending to her will. She still had her hooks in me.

"You know what, you're right," I said swallowing my pride. " I had a girlfriend at the time. I had no reason to get upset."

"Are you guys still together?" she asked trying not to sound too interested.

"Nah, we broke up."

"Who broke up with who? Did you break up with her, or did she break up with you?"

"Why does that matter?"

"It just does. So, who broke up with who?"

"I broke up with her. So, you missed me?"

"Maybe…a little," she said coyly again.

"We should hang-out. For old times sake," I said. "What are you doing this weekend?"

"Nothing."

"Let's go out to dinner."

"Okay."

And just like that I was back on the chain gang.

That weekend I decided to take Rainy to the Grill. I thought it would impress her. And it did. She really got off on that whole downtown scene. Even though we had to wait 45 minutes for our food to show up, she thought it was the greatest place on earth. Our waitress was some tattooed broad named Lyn. She was a casual acquaintance of Roo's and had waited on us numerous times. I wasn't sure if she recognized me or not, but I hoped she didn't.

Sitting there in that lumpy red vinyl booth with the duct tape covering it's wounds I couldn't help but think of Roo. I still missed her at times and felt guilty about how I had treated her. But it was all in the past now. I had to just keep going forward. It was detrimental to spend too much time wallowing in the past. You had to forget and move on.

Sitting there with Rainy I couldn't believe my incredible luck. Things were going great. Rainy was laughing at my jokes. We were flirting with each other. I felt like I was on top of the world. I hadn't felt this good in awhile. It was moments like this that kept me going. You never knew what life had in store for you. One day you could be living on skid row and the next in a penthouse apartment. Life was funny that way. If it wasn't for knowing that unexpected luck could strike you at any time, I probably would have offed myself long ago.

After dinner, I stopped by a grocery store, and picked up a couple bottles of wine before we went back to my place. When we got there, I put Sade on the record player and let the wine work it's magic (they should file Sade under panty dropper at the record store; if a girl even remotely likes you it's a guarantee her clothes are coming off).

It wasn't long before the wine and music started to take an effect and me and Rainy were all over each other. We were like two velociraptors in heat. My pulse quickened and in a blur we went from my couch to the floor. We tore at each other's clothes and my member throbbed in anticipation. I let my hands slide all over her body like snakes. The dam of sexual tension, that had been building between us, was about to burst. I was standing at the gates of heaven ready to dive in. I was certain this would be the sexual encounter of a life time. As far as I was concerned, all my life had merely been a build up to this point. Castles would fall and angels would weep at this moment. I raised my sword high in the air and plunged it deep betwixt Rainy's thighs. It sank quick and true –to the hilt. I pulled it out and thrust again, over and over, repeatedly gaining my rhythm.

But something was wrong.

I slowed down, disappointed and disheartened. My dreams were quickly giving way to reality. I had been fooled. Rainy wasn't the great lover I had anticipated her to be. As a matter of fact, it was like fucking a cardboard cut-out. Or a mannequin. She just laid there stiff and rigid. I tried letting her get on top, but that was even worse. She had no rhythm. She floundered on my dick like a dying fish. It was terrible. How could someone so hot, be so bad in bed? It's not like she was a virgin.

I grabbed her hips and manually worked her back and forth on my cock, her tits flopping this way and that, until I came. It was the worse screw ever. But what could you expect from someone in high school?

Post coitus, Rainy nestled in my arms, I stared up at the roof thinking about how bad the sex was. I was dumbfounded. I should have saw it for the omen that it was, a precursor to the terrible things that had yet to come, but I didn't. Instead I got up, went to the kitchen and poured myself a glass of juice. Orange with extra pulp. It was cold and refreshing going down my throat. Me and Rainy were officially a couple.

Chapter 25
(late February)

Being with Rainy wasn't what I had anticipated it to be. And the longer we were together the more evident and acute her issues and insecurities became.

Her New York fantasy became an obsession. She told me constantly that she planned to leave in a year to pursue her dreams of acting, and that I shouldn't get too attached. It was a crock of shit though. I knew she would never leave, and I think she did too. I suspect the only reason she would say this, or one of the main reasons, was to try and cause me stress. She knew I was crazy about her and I suspect, subconsciously, that she was trying to use this against me, as a way to gain control.

Also, once we were an official couple she became extremely jealous, and constantly suspected me of cheating. She said she had trouble trusting men due to her father taking off, but I suspected it had more to do with her mom brainwashing her into believing all men are scum.

As a result, she started asking to check my cell phone call-history, on a regular basis. Since I had nothing to hide, I readily acquiesced. I would submit to anything to keep her from plunging into one of her sullen moods, which could take anywhere from hours to days for her to come out of.

All these things (and more) had slowly been coming to my realization over the last month or so, as I had gotten to know Rainy better. A smarter man would have headed for the hills and got the fuck out of town, but love blinded me. I couldn't see the forest for the trees. I know what it was –I was in love with the idea of her. The fantasy I had created. I had saw Rainy and made up a story (in my mind) to go along with the image. I had turned her into something she wasn't, into something I wanted her to be, something no person could ever be –perfect. That was bad habit of mine. I made women out to be the answers to all my problems, then I was let down when they didn't live up to it. It was something I seriously needed to work on. But it was too late now. I was already hooked.

Instead I spent my time trying to keep Rainy happy, which was no small feat. There was always something upsetting her. She gave new meaning to the words, "high maintenance".

Case in point, we went to a carnival one night and Rainy insisted that I win her one of the largest teddy bears they had. Why she wanted one of those cheap knock-offs, stuffed with oily rags, and made by some poor kid in a third world country, I'll never know. Perhaps it was supposed to stand as a symbol of our love. All I know is, it was my responsibility to win her one.

Now, I've never claimed to be athletic, but a gold-medal Olympian would have struggled to beat these games. They were all fucking rigged: toss and land pennies on a greased plate, sink a basket with a ball too large for the hoop, use a baseball to knock over milk-bottles that have been glued to the table, they were all cons.

And the worst part about this whole farce was, trying to achieve the impossible while being mocked by some toothless carnie as he stood there lusting after Rainy's tight body (barely covered with clothes), like he couldn't decide which one of her holes he wanted to stick his dick in first. Not to mention the fact, that I had to pay for all this!

Needless to say, it was one failed attempt after the other. Rainy saw this as a direct result of my lack of love for her, and grew increasingly annoyed with each failed attempt. By the time we left she wasn't speaking to me and I was $75 in the hole. To appease her

I had to stop by a toy store, on the way home, and buy her the biggest teddy bear I could find.

Unfortunately, shit like this was an every day occurrence, rather than the rare exception. But it was either this or the confinement of solitude. I decided to stick it out. I thought maybe I could change her. Or perhaps, we were just getting off to a rocky start and that calmer waters lie ahead. What did I know?

Chapter 26
(mid March)

Flowers were waking from their winter slumber. Kits, cubs and whelps were taking their first steps. Spring was in the air and it was time for prom. That magical time when young maidens come into bloom only to be deflowered. And Rainy, like most of her female contemporaries, was obsessed with what she'd wear.

I, on the other hand, was worried about who she might be attending this gala with. I flat-out refused to go. I still had *some* dignity left and I'd be damned if I was gonna be caught doing the Cabbage Patch at some high school prom. Yet, at the same time, I didn't want her going with the captain of the football team, or whoever else might ask her. It was a sticky predicament.

Luckily for me, Rainy decided to go with her best friend. A closet homosexual by the name of Timothy. She told me I had nothing to worry about as they were just friends. And I told her I had nothing to worry about on the account that he was gay. She said just because he was in her drama class that didn't make him gay. I said that I agreed completely, but the fact that he wore eyeliner and bangle bracelets probably did.

Anyway, for two whole weeks I was dragged from dress shop, to dress shop. It was a complete nightmare. I didn't like the person I was becoming. I was becoming a henpecked pussy. Here I was sitting on dressing room couches, holding Rainy's purse, as she played dress-up. What had happened to me? I had been edgier than this. I felt like a neutered tom-cat. Instead of carousing and caterwauling, in seedy back alleys, I now sat on the porch and left it to the other felines. I was getting soft.

The only saving grace was, one afternoon while at the mall, Rainy let me fuck her in a Victoria's Secret dressing room. I bent her over, hiked up her skirt, and slid it in. It was hot. I mean, real kinky shit. The only thing separating my thrusting cock from good ol' American commerce was a thin curtain. I'm certain the sales girl had to hear us, or smell the scent of pussy, but no one tried to interrupt us. Maybe this was a common occurrence at Victoria Secret's. I don't know.

In the end, Rainy ended up wearing what looked like a wedding gown, the fairy wings from her Halloween Tinker-Bell costume, and a tiara from one of her old pageants to prom. It was a little over the top, if you ask me, and just more shit for me to take off when she came over to my place to get fucked that night.

After prom, when she got to my apartment, I had to listen (for over an hour) how everyone simply loved Her and Timothy's attire. Apparently she had found him some matching black wings to compliment hers. She said they matched his tux perfectly and he absolutely loved them (and yet she was certain of his hetero status). It appears everyone at prom couldn't stop fawning over them and their unique style. She said that the outdoor venue, underneath the stars, had been purely magical, and the only thing that could have made it better is if I had been there.

I had to agree. It would have been better if I was there (for Rainy at least). And seeing how the outdoor venue was actually the zoo, I imagined it had been pretty magical. Everyone knows that the smell of rhino shit and tiger farts make for an enchanting evening.

As I sat there listening to her recap her night, I suddenly started to wonder what I was doing in a relationship with a high school girl. Is this really where I wanted to be? And for the first time, instead of viewing Rainy as "miss right", I started thinking of her as "miss right now".

Chapter 27
(April)

Everyone at work had decided to get together one night to go to the bar across the street. I didn't have any intention of attending until Rainy insisted she was going. Seeing how she was such a social butterfly, and talked to everyone at work, she was always invited to the "grown-up" events all the other baggers were left out of. And since Roberta (the cashier who had thrown the Halloween party), was good friends with the door-man, she said she could get Rainy in even though she was under-age.

It was a safe bet all the horny guys from work would be there, and that they'd all be drunk. I wasn't gonna take the chance of another "bathroom incident", like the one that happened in December, taking place. I begrudgingly had to go.

I tried to talk Rainy into the idea of a quiet evening at my place, but she wasn't having it. All I wanted to do is go home and get high after work. I didn't want to have to socialize with everyone from my job. But there was no way out of it. And since I didn't want to be there, I showed up in a bad mood.

As I entered the dingy tavern across the street, I forced a smile on my face and greeted everyone of my co-workers I came across, as I pushed my way to the bar. I ordered a shot of whiskey with a beer back. I had to get my head straight before I could be expected to handle this bag of shit. I slammed the first and took long swigs from the latter, and made my way over to Rainy and the table of people she was sitting with. Rainy had got there about a half hour earlier than me on the account she was off that day, and I was wondering what had transpired during the time she was out of my site. How many guys had hit on her? How many had she flirted with? I was growing increasingly annoyed.

I saw Brad, from the "bathroom incident", standing in the corner and I gave him a dirty look. Every since that night he had become my sworn enemy. I couldn't bear to look at him. It burned my eyes. He was the very personification of my shame and embarrassment –my inadequacy.

I sat down, pouted, and drank my beer. Rainy was in an exceptionally good mood. She thrived in these environments. She loved gatherings and parties. I somehow always felt sapped in these conditions. Rainy seemed oblivious to my plight, or she simply ignored it. She had no regard for my feelings. I grew sullen and decided I needed to get very drunk. I stood up and headed toward the bar.

While I went to the bar to get another beer and whiskey, Darren (one of the low-level dickhead managers from up front), came up and asked Rainy to dance. It was common knowledge me and Rainy were an item. Did he want to die?

As I watched them dance, like a couple of offbeat honkies, I could feel my temperature rising. I wanted blood. Now, I'm not a violent man, but in a fit of rage I feel I could be capable of the most heinous acts. I truly understand what they mean when they say a crime of passion. My instincts said to smash the beer bottle in my hand, and use it as a knife to slash Darren's face. I could imagine the blood splattered mess as the meat hung loosely from his cheeks. The image comforted me. But it was impractical. There were too many people around and I would undoubtedly get fired for such an act. I wasn't positive, but I was pretty sure that McKipson's frowned upon dismembering a member of management's face with a broken beer bottle, whether it was on company property or not.

Instead I told the bartender to make it a double and left. I drove around uncertain of what to do. I felt disrespected and humiliated. I don't think I had ever been so mad. I wanted to go back and drag Rainy out of that bar by her hair. But in lieu of committing battery, I went down the street to Temptations Show Club, got piss drunk, and paid a cracked-out stripper a hundred bucks to give me a blowjob in the v.i.p. room. Then I ignored Rainy's calls for the next couple of days. It was typical passive aggressive behavior, but at least it made me feel better at the time.

Chapter 28
(late May)

It was hot and I was sweaty and I felt like a stooge, sitting there in the bleachers all by myself, but it meant a lot to Rainy, so there I was. Linda was sitting somewhere else with grandma and grandpa. It was graduation day.

After 13 years of schooling Rainy was finally free. And we were all there to congratulate her. Her dad had even come down from Oregon with his new family. Not so much to congratulate his daughter, as to get Linda to sign a piece of paper stating Rainy was now eighteen and out of high school, therefore he was no longer legally bound to keep sending child support. *Yeah*, he was a real sweetheart. I could tell rainy wasn't keen on having him there (she knew why he had shown up), and as a result she had been extra bitchy all week long. I bore the brunt of it.

It seemed like this was quickly becoming my new job. I was Rainy's official door mat. I had never been treated this way by a woman. Usually I was the one doing the shitting. For the first time in my life I was getting shit on. Maybe this was God's way of teaching me a lesson. Every time something went wrong in Rainy's life, no matter how trivial, somehow I was to blame. Some of the things that would send her into hysterics I found completely astounding. A stubbed toe would become the reason for hour long laments. I felt sorry for her. She was gonna have a long hard life if this was the way she reacted to everything. She acted like she was the only person on earth that bad shit happened to. Like everybody else's life was a bunch of fucking roses. It was ridiculous. All I can say is, it's amazing what I'll put myself through for a set of D-cups, a tiny waist, and an ass like a peach.

As far as graduations go, it was pretty common fare. The school wheeled out it's valedictorians to give their typical, corny, "the future is ours" speech. Yes, that was an "s" at the end of valedictorian, indicating plural, it appears too many people were crying that it was unfair to have just one, since often the differences separating the winning student from the runner-ups is small and sometimes unfair acts, like taking extra easy courses to get additional credits; personally I saw it as the further weakening of America's youths, this whole "we're all winners" mentality where everyone gets a trophy at the end of the season is bullshit –what happened to, "to the victor go the spoils", and besides, valedictorians are a bunch of fucking shit bags anyway, why would you even want to be one, they end up running corrupt companies that rape the land and the common man, so fuck the schools and their valedictorians, I say. And of course the principal was on hand to dole out the pearls of wisdom he's gained over the years, which consisted of a dusted off copy of last year's cliché address to the graduating student body. Overall, it was pretty depressing. Here I was, five years out of high school and what had I accomplished?

NOTHING!

I should have been working on a master's degree by this point. Instead I was chasing high school poon. What a waste!

After the ceremony, when everyone had thrown their caps into the air, I made my way down to the football field and congratulated Rainy personally. I met her father for the first time (a tall goon with about as much personality as Linda) and took the obligatory high school graduation pictures with Rainy.

Afterwards, I took Rainy to a fancy restaurant in the foothills specializing in Pacific Rim fusion cuisine, to celebrate. I should have known better. I should have stuck to Arby's. Like I said, the presence of Rainy's father had put her in an especially foul mood, even for her. I guess her father showing up in a brand new car, yet saying he was a little strapped for cash at the moment and he would have to get her a graduation present later, didn't really help matters.

In typical Rainy fashion, she blew a gasket when the place didn't have ranch dressing for her fresh Thai salad with edamame and peanut sauce. I told her as soon as she ordered it they wouldn't have ranch dressing, knowing full well that's what she would want, but she went ahead and ordered it anyway. Then she insisted that I ask the waitress, on her behalf, if they had ranch. Of course the waitress looked at me like I was retarded for even asking such a stupid question. And somehow the whole thing became my fault. Suddenly, I was to blame for Thailand's lack of ranch dressing. As if there had been fountains of it flowing until I showed up, conquered the country, and usurped all the creamy goodness that is ranch dressing, hoarding it for myself. I couldn't win. I sat staring at my spring rolls and chicken pad thai, wondering how many dates it would take to get in the waitress' pants.

Chapter 29
(June)

Spring quickly gave way to summer, and the mercury began it's annual climb to the top of the thermometer, as usual. The summers in Tucson are always unbearable. You can literally spit on the sidewalk and hear it sizzle. The only saving grace is the fact that the University clears out, and all the trust-fund-babies go back to wherever they came from. You can actually have lunch at a bar on 4th avenue, without being swarmed by cunts named Buffy and dicks named Chad. The college kids are like ants at a picnic and the hot Arizona summers are the blessed poison granules sent to set us free. But I digress.

A lot of changes had taken place in the last few months: me and Rainy had officially got together, Rainy had graduated high school, and the most significant of all, Linda had bought Rainy her own place –a small down-stairs unit in a housing co-op. It wasn't a palace or anything, but still, it was her own place! I would have killed for my own place when I was her age. I guess Linda thought it was time for Rainy to leave the nest.

She said it would be a great learning experience and help teach Rainy the meaning of responsibility. I thought it was a little premature seeing how Rainy wasn't even capable of keeping her room clean, but as I've said before, what did I know.

Those weren't the only events to transpire though. The day after graduation, Andy told Rainy he was promoting her to bakery as a reward for all her hard work.

Everyday after work she would come home smelling like donuts, cake, frosting and all other manner of baked goods. Not to mention, the dye in the frosting stained the tips of her fingers red, blue, yellow and green. It was like fucking the Pillsbury Dough Boy and getting hand-jobs from a rainbow.

Yes, everything was looking on the up and up. Even me and Rainy seemed to be getting along better. Then, as seems to be the way things go in my life, the bottom dropped out.

Chapter 30
(July)

I had been feeling pretty restless at my job the last couple of months. Everyday it was

the same fucking thing. The same people, the same customers, the same everything. That's how they get you. It's like marriage. You get in a fucking routine, you get comfortable, and after a while you're like, "Fuck it! I've been here this long!" Well, not this cowboy. I had had enough. I couldn't take anymore. Everyday I left work feeling like my best parts had failed to been engaged. I was rusting from the inside out. I had to get out of there one way or another.

I couldn't just quit though. Not without being provoked. Quitting without being provoked would just be proving what everybody thought, that I was a lazy bum with no direction. Well, fuck that! I wanted to be a martyr! The patron saint of slackers everywhere! My provocation came two weeks later in the form of an idiot customer.

By this time I had come to the conclusion that most of the public was border line retarded, and somehow they thought it was your fault.

This toothless hillbilly, who decided to fuck with me, was a perfect example. He walked up smelling like Old Milwaukee and Skoal.

"Where'dja put the sara-deans?" he asked.

I wasn't sure I heard him right. His lack of teeth made it hard to discern his rambling.

"I'm sorry sir, what are you looking for?"

"Sara-deans! Where'dja put the sara-deans?" he said growing impatient.

"I didn't put the sara-deans anywhere. I don't think we even carry sara-deans."

Now he really started to get annoyed. Somehow it was my fault because I had never heard of sara-deans before. As if it was my responsibility to memorize the eating habits of the upper-Appalachian mountain-man. I figured it was probably some salty processed pork product designed to pickle your insides. Or from the state of his mouth, some corn-syrup concoction (heavy on red dye no. 4) created to rot your teeth from the inside out. I wanted to tell him to go fuck a goat, but I couldn't risk getting in anymore trouble. I had to swallow my pride and try to discern this caveman's request.

"You tryin' to tell me yall don't carry sara-deans!"

"What are sara-deans, sir?"

"Ya know, sara-deans! Those little fish in the can, Jesus Christ boy!"

Little fish in the can? Sara-deans?

Oh, shit!

This motherfucker means, sardines!

"*Oh*, you mean *SARDINES*. Well, *SARDINES* are on aisle seven. We have *SARDINES* in mustard. *SARDINES* in oil. We have all kinds of *SARDINES* over there, sir. If you like I can take you over and show you the *SARDINES*."

"Naw, I think I can manage, smart ass."

It was shit like this that ate me up. Having to demean myself because of other people's ignorance. I could feel the lava boiling up inside me. I snapped.

"Well do me a favor, next time before you come in here, learn to speak proper English you fuck-tard!

The red-neck's eye's grew large in astonishment as he stomped off, huffing and puffing. I guess he wasn't use to people talking to him that way. Less than a minute later Andy was calling me into his office. I found him sitting at his desk, writing something down. He didn't bother to look up.

"You know Vincente, you say you care about this job, but I just don't see it. You show up late every day, you drag your feet along like you don't give a shit, and most of your time is spent fraternizing with the female employees. And if that wasn't bad enough, now you are insulting customers on a regular basis."

I couldn't believe my fucking ears. What the hell had happened to this guy? Who in the hell had emasculated him along the way? He was in his 20's for crying out loud. The only thing he should've been concerned with was getting laid and wasted everyday.

I could feel the hostility brewing inside me. I was like a kettle ready to blow. Who in the hell did this punk think he was? I was already fed up with this job, I didn't need his shit on top of it. I snapped and cut him off before he could go any further.

"You know what Andy, save your shit. I don't need it. Give it to the next guy, you fucking tool," I said walking out of his office.

Andy's jaw dropped. He wasn't expecting that one. But you know what the sad part was? I envied him. Deep down I really wanted to be like him. Just another mindless drone. Someone happy to be lining someone else's pocket. Why couldn't I be that guy? The guy that didn't see the bigger picture. No, I always wanted more. I wanted to be special. I guess some people are just born to be puppets. Me, I wanted to be king. As Hemingway said, intelligent people suffer most. I guess ignorance, truly is bliss.

At any rate, it felt great to just walk out like that and turn my back on the establishment. It was like telling the world to kiss my ass. I felt alive for the first time, in a long time. But like all things, it was short lived.

Chapter 31
(July)

At first Rainy was happy to hear I quit. She knew how miserable I was at that job.

"Good baby, I'm glad you quit. You're too smart for that place." Those were her exact words. I guess she thought I was going to go out and get a job that paid me a 100g's a year now. Boy, was she mistaken. I wasn't trained to do anything else. Other than bagging groceries, working in the deli was the only thing I had ever done. What kind of job could I be expected to land?

So, instead of looking for a gig, I sat around for about a month doing nothing. It was nice to finally have *the man* off my back. Since I had been in the 401k plan at work and had managed to save up a little money on the side, I was okay on cash –for a little while . I merely cashed out my 401k and spent my afternoons laying around and reading.

But my life of leisure didn't last long. Before I knew it, I only had a hundred and fifty dollars left to my name, and a month and a half left on my lease. I tried breaking it, but the cock-suckers who owned the place said I would still have to pay the last month. It was in the contract. I had no other choice but to start selling off my furniture to pay the last month's rent. Not that it mattered. Soon I wasn't gonna have a place to put it in anyway. This all put me in a very compromising position. I had to think fast. The way I looked at it I had two choices: Move home with my parents, or kiss Rainy's ass and hope she let me stay with her. The latter seemed the least degrading of the two, so I opted for it. Luckily it worked.

I knew Rainy wouldn't allow me to sit around on my ass, reading, while she went to work though, so I had to find a job. Which suited me just fine. My working-class, Chicano, upbringing was starting to kick in. And once that happens you have no choice but to find a job. The only problem was, nothing paid well. I was tired of working menial jobs that didn't pay shit. I had had my taste of it and didn't care for it. Writing. Now that seemed like a career. Those guy's had found a way to beat the system. From what I could gather, they were just a bunch of tortured drunks and addicts (the good one's anyway), who got wasted all day and wrote. That seemed like the life to me. These brilliant individuals became my new heroes.

After selling off most my shit, I was able to pay my last months rent, and still have enough change left over to keep me out of the poor house for a little while. The few earthly possessions, I had left, I put into a storage unit as I prepared to move in with Rainy. It was the end of an era. And the beginning of something new.

Chapter 32
(August)

Living with Rainy definitely took some getting used to. I wasn't accustomed to being a kept man. Which is basically what I was. I didn't pay any of the bills, or bring home the bacon, which is what I had been raised to believe men do –provide. So, needless to say, this new role I was filling left me with ambivalent feelings.

But after a while, (I'm ashamed to admit this) I started to like it. It was nice not having the pressure of making the rent and all the other bills associated with maintaining a house-hold. I'd watch Rainy sweating bullets, wondering how she was going to make ends meet, and laugh. I don't know who the fuck she thought she was kidding, playing grown-up. Her mom is the one who paid the rent. Rainy spent all her money on cigarettes, make-up, and cute little outfits to squeeze her hot ass into. These theatrics and melodrama seemed to add some trivial significance to her life though, so I always played along, and offered to help out anyway I could.

I wasn't a moocher, though. I did my part. Rainy worked 11a.m. to 7p.m. So during that time I would clean house, wash the dishes, go grocery shopping, make dinner, and do laundry. I even bought a couple of rose bushes (with the little money I had left) for me to tend to. I was like fucking Donna Reed and June Cleaver all wrapped up into one manly package. Rainy hardly ever noticed, but I didn't give a care, I was doing it more for me than her. She lived like a fucking slob. I couldn't stand to wallow around in her filth. It also gave me something to throw in her face if she said I wasn't helping out.

But it wasn't enough for Rainy. She started to get frustrated with me. She said I had to stop being so damn proud and just take whatever I could get. I had an offer to work in another grocery store, but that's the last thing I wanted. I had clawed tooth and nail to get out of that predicament. Going back to it would just be admitting defeat. Admitting that was all I was cut out to do.

About this time Rainy's mom turned on me, as well. Not that she had ever been my biggest fan, but now that I was out of work and having difficulties, I was lower than low. Occasionally Linda would come over to inspect the condition of the house. See where her money was going. She'd blow in like a tornado, raise a lot of dust, and just stare at me. She wouldn't say hi, boo, eat shit, nothing. She hated me and thought I was Mexican trash. It ate her up inside to know that I went to sleep with one of her daughter's pink nipples in my mouth every night. When ever she came over I made sure to have a beer in my hand. I know that pissed her off. I'd even go as far as pretending to be a little drunk. She wouldn't even acknowledge my presence in the room. I'd have to make myself noticed.

"Oh, hi Linda. Rainy didn't say you were coming over. You want a beer?"

"No thank you, Vincente." She'd hiss.

"Oh, ok. Well if you're hungry I think there is half a sandwich left in the fridge."

She would just glare at me after that. Boy, if looks could kill! Rainy would tell me her mom liked me, but I wasn't fucking stupid.

To tell you the truth though, Linda wasn't that bad. She just liked bitching and crying about what jerks men are, and how they had done her wrong. She was bitter. After all, her looks were gone, she didn't have any personality, and she was all alone. I figured if it wasn't me she was pissed at, it would be someone else. Fuck it. I'd carry that cross for awhile.

At any rate, Linda started telling Rainy I was a dead-beat who would never amount to anything. Rainy disagreed, at first. But her confidence in me was starting to wane. I now had opposition facing me from all corners. It was more than I could handle. My immune system began to weaken. I started feeling rundown and tired all the time. My joints ached and I started to suffer from panic attacks and depression. Weed and booze was no longer enough to escape from reality. I needed something stronger. I went to my drug dealer.

Chapter 33
(August)

I had a couple of different guys I bought drugs from. One guy was this Jewish gangster I had been introduced to, by a friend of my cousin. He lived in Barrio Hollywood, drove around a cherried-out '69 Lincoln Continental, packed a nine millimeter, and had all kinds of scary Hebrew tattoos; like the word LODZ (the name of the ghetto his grandparents had been confined to) across one set of knuckles, and the word KIKE across the other set. But despite his appearance he was a real laid back guy. He was pretty fucking smart, too. Me and him would sit around for hours just getting high and bullshitting. He knew every thing you could ever want to know about cars, and I'd often ask him for motor advice.

The other guy was this obnoxious weasel, I basically couldn't stand. I only used him as my back-up, when I couldn't get a hold of my Hebrew homie. His name was Rico and he dressed like a yuppie, drove nice cars, and lived in an expensive condo equipped with security cameras to watch his shit. He thought he was Tucson's answer to Don Juan. He represented everything I despised in the world. He was annoying, skinny and arrogant. Not to mention, he always had some hot piece of druggie ass hanging around. It made me sick. Or maybe jealous is a better word. I knew the chicks were only using him for his shit, but it didn't matter. Take all his nice stuff away, and what did he have that I didn't have? Sure, maybe I was a little thick around the middle and enjoyed watching cartoons, but who doesn't?

The only redeeming quality about this guy was he got killer weed, and he never weighed a sack. He merely crammed weed in a sandwich bag and asked for twenty bucks in return. He didn't care. For him, it was another way to show off. Plus he knew he would always make it up on coke, pills, and the various other narcotics he peddled. If it wasn't for that I wouldn't have had anything to do with the fucking parasite. He was always trying to turn me on to new shit. Turn me into one of his little junkies. He had people all over town who owed him the shirt off their back. Whatever you wanted he always had, or could get in a couple of days. Weed, coke, E, meth, opium, acid, special K, uppers, downers, H, prescriptions. I wasn't interested in any of those chemicals he had though. I was all about the natural stuff. The stuff I thought was safe. I wanted mushrooms.

I had never tried mushrooms, but all the pot-heads I knew swore they were the shit. They said it was just like being really high for a few hours. That sounded like harmless fun to me.

I knocked on Rico's door and he invited me in, trying to act all brotherly, like we were old friends or something. He had an old playboy on the coffee table so I picked it up and flipped through the pages. The chicks looked good, but unreal. Too perfect. Bleach-blond bimbos with hard plastic tits and airbrushed bodies. I preferred my women with a little meat on their bones. A little cellulite never hurt anyone. Not that I'd kick a playboy model out of bed, but you get what I mean.

"What's up Vincent! What you need man? You smoke all that weed already?"

"Nah, I still got some. I wanted to ask you about something else. You got any shrooms?"

"Oh shit! Movin' up I see. My man wants to try some shrooms."

"Cut the shit, Rico. So do you got any, or what?"

"Yeah, I got some man. How much you need?"

"I don't know. Give me enough for about three different trips."

"All right."

He went to his freezer and pulled out a big zip-loc bag full of caps and stems. He started putting them on the scale.

"This is good shit, right? This ain't that crap laced with speed, is it?" I asked.

"Man! I only sell good shit!"

"Sure you do."

Chapter 34
(August)

After I scored I rushed home to Rainy. I thought this would be a perfect opportunity for us to do some bonding. She came home after work and we started to wolf them down. I split the stash into thirds, I took a third, Rainy took a third, and I put the other third away for safe keeping. We sat down on the couch and put some cartoons on the television.

It took about an hour for them to kick in, and when they did, I wasn't impressed. I saw some vivid colors and that was about the extent of it. I decided I needed to help things along. I pulled out my bong and me and Rainy smoked a couple bowls, then I finished off the remaining shrooms. Now, I've done some pretty stupid things in my life, but that was probably the stupidest. It all hit me at once. Like Alice, I was falling down the rabbit hole –tumbling. And in case you don't know, you should never chase rabbits.

It was pure fear. A sensory overload. I felt like I was losing my mind. The more you tried to control it the more you realized you couldn't. It was like your mind was racing through time and space and exploding into another dimension. I got scared I'd never feel normal again. The trip ebbed and flowed like water. High peaks followed by deep plunges, brief instances of stillness, then another high peak and a plunge. A psychedelic rollercoaster. Rainy could see the fear in my eyes and it began to spook her. Seeing her scared, scared me more, and we fed off each other's fear. I started to doubt reality and wondered if anything was real. It was everything you had ever heard about a bad trip. I thought for sure I was going to crack and they would put my ass in a mental ward for the rest of my life. That scared me to death. I could see myself walking around in a hospital gown, painting the walls with crude pictures made out of my own shit.

I managed to collect myself for a few seconds and told Rainy I was sleepy and wanted to go to bed. She knew I was full of shit but thought we should go to bed too. I figured if I could just go to bed, I could sleep it off. In the morning I would be fine. It wasn't that easy though.

Me and Rainy went to our sides of the bed and held on for dear life. After what seemed like forever, I fell asleep, and had terrible nightmares. The drugs were working on my mind at warp speed, forcing me to use parts of my brain people don't use for specific biological reasons. I was plunged deeper, and deeper into my own psyche. I saw myself slowly floating through space, clinging to a broken asteroid, the sole survivor of some cataclysmic disaster. I was all alone. No one but me and the infinite darkness of space. The drugs were playing on my sub-conscious, bringing my darkest fears to light. My deepest fear was being alone. Having nobody love me.

All of a sudden I had a moment of clarity, an epiphany. That's why I clung to women. They gave me a false sense of security. But it never lasted. In the end I would still be alone. No one but me.

Relief came with the dawn. I was elated. I had survived. I woke Rainy up so we could compare stories. She thought my trip was heavier than hers. She had only experienced nasty visuals, mine was a shamanistic journey which led to self discovery. I was like fucking Jim Morrison, or something. Regardless I had learned my lesson. The human mind was not something to be tampered with. I was going straight. I threw away my bong, my pipes, my papers, and my weed. It felt great. I was a free man. No more monkey on my back. I was going to be a happy, productive, member of society. I opened up the fridge to get a drink of water –pure refreshing water. A bottle of rum and a six pack of beer stared back at me.

I pulled them out and walked over to the sink.

"I should throw these away," I thought, "I don't need this anymore. I'm gonna stand on my own two feet."

Then I heard a voice deep inside me, "Easy tiger! Don't get carried away. It's going to be a long life."

I put the booze back in the fridge, being careful not to break it in the process, then grabbed the water. It was cold and tasted good.

Chapter 35
(September)

Me and Rainy's bad trip had brought us closer together, but the relationship still wasn't out of the woods yet. It was a month later and I still hadn't found a job. And worse yet, my anxiety and panic attacks seemed to be getting more severe. In an attempt to self-medicate I started drinking every night. During the day, while Rainy was at work, I spent all my time reading and laying in bed. I had stopped playing house frau, long ago, and the rose bushes I had bought lay withered and dead on the porch. I didn't care anymore. I was officially broke and penniless. I was a deadbeat. Rainy had officially lost hope in me and so had I. Even though I felt like a loser, I just couldn't bring myself to take a job, or do anything else for that matter.

Before me and Roo broke up she had given me a copy of *Women* by Charles Bukowski. For the last few months it had been sitting in a corner, unread. I hadn't even bothered to crack open the cover. Then one day I happen to see it laying there. I picked it up and thumbed through the pages. In the back of the book was a picture of the author. He looked like a craggy old cliff side, weathered and unmovable. I started to read. It was unlike anything I had ever read. The sentences were simple and sweet. They jumped off the page and kicked like a mule. There wasn't any time wasted mincing words. It grabbed a hold of you and demanded that you pay attention; so few books do that. Reading it I didn't feel quite as crazy anymore. This Bukowski cat was ten times as fucked up as me. It was one of the greatest books I had ever read. It changed my idea of what literature could be. It made me think, maybe I could take a crack at this writing thing.

But as good as Bukowski was, he wasn't enough to get me out of this funk I was in. Things had really gotten bad. I mean, I had just lost my job of eight years, I was living with a bitchy girlfriend, I didn't have any money, I was drinking heavily, I had recently kicked a three year marijuana habit (and was having difficulties coping without), and I kept feeling like I was about to go crazy. My life was spiraling deeper and deeper down the crapper.

Rainy suggested I see a shrink. She had seen this woman when she was younger and said it really seemed to help. I thought, what the hell, it's worth a try. I was tired of feeling alone. Feeling that there was nothing and no one I could relate to. Everywhere I went I saw people who appeared to be in control and have life figured out. I wanted to be one of them. I asked my mom for a small loan to pay for the visit and made an appointment. The doctor was able to fit me in a week later.

Chapter 36
(September)

I showed up nervous and paranoid. It was kind of weird going to see a psychiatrist. Especially since my girlfriend used to see this lady when she was a kid. But I was serious about the healing process. I tried to not let it bother me.

The doctor's name was Vivian Dwight. She was in her late forties, early fifties, and she still looked pretty good. She was one of those ladies you could tell took care of herself (of course it is easy to take care of yourself when you have money, everything is easier when you have money). She had nice legs. Solid calves and thighs. Plump, round, breasts. And pretty green eyes. It was her hands and face that gave her away. You could tell that she had broken some hearts in her day and been a real sweetheart. I wished I had known her back then. Not that she would have had anything to do with me, but it is always nice to know an attractive woman. A pretty face can ease a lot of things.

The Dr. asked that I take a seat on her couch and make myself comfortable. I lowered myself on the couch. It wasn't like the movies where you had to lie down. Instead you sat there, while she sat across from you. I was disappointed.

"So what brings you here?" she asked me.

I took a deep breath and exhaled through my nose. I started to tell her about how Rainy recommend I come, and how therapy had helped her, but somewhere along the line it became a forum for what a bitch I thought Linda was. I went on and on. Not caring what I said.

I told Dr. Dwight that I thought Rainy was spoiled. That her mom had brought her up wrong and fucked up her head. I also told her that I thought Rainy had a twisted view of reality, lived in a fantasy world, thought everyone was here to serve her, had a tendency to flip-out whenever the tiniest thing didn't go her way, and that it came as no surprise to me that she had been a patient of the good doctor some years earlier.

"Why would you stay with someone whom you have such negative feelings towards?" the doctor asked.

"I don't know," I said. "I just seem to be attracted to girls who walk all over me…I guess the main reason I stay with Rainy is because I think she's gorgeous."

The doctor found this very interesting. She asked me to elaborate.

I told her that I viewed Rainy as a trophy. That I liked the way she looked hanging off my arm. The attention she got me.

"Besides," I said. "if I broke up with Rainy I would have to move back in with my parents. And I rather hang myself than move back home. That would mean I was a complete failure."

Dr. Dwight seemed a little taken back by my candor. I could tell she wasn't accustom to this kind of honesty so early in a first session. I didn't care. The only way I thought she could help me was if I was brutally honest with her. I was paying this woman too much money (a hundred dollars an hour) to beat around the bush.

Unfortunately, after my little diatribe on Rainy, my time was up. I couldn't believe it. It had gone by too fast. I still had a lot to say. But the clock ruled the room.

The doctor took my money, thanked me, and asked if I would like to make another appointment. I seriously contemplated the question in my head. It felt liberating to get all that shit off my chest, but at the same time I felt as if I had gotten nowhere. I hadn't even had a chance to bring up my anxiety attacks or all my other quirks. I might as well have wiped my ass with that hundred dollars. I felt like I had just been conned. Damn, I could have bought a fat sack of weed with that kind of money and smoked all my problems away. I tried to calm myself down and remember that the healing process was long and arduous. Rome wasn't built in a day. I said sure and made an appointment for the same time next week.

I showed up to the next session a little frazzled and determined to make some progress. It had been a rough week. I wanted to cut through all the bullshit and get down to the root of the problem. I wanted to find out what was wrong with me. Why sometimes, all of a sudden, I felt like I was dying. Why I felt like I was cracking-up. Why I was scared all the time. I walked into the Doctor's office and took a seat.

"Good afternoon, Vincente," she said.

"Hello," I answered.

She looked back down at her notebook and continued to write. Cool as coconut cream pie. I got a little angry. She had barely even acknowledged me. I felt like she could care less if I got the helped I needed. All I was to her was a walking pay-check.

"Goddamn", I thought, "this woman is worse than a whore."

At least you leave a whore feeling gratified. As if you accomplished something. This woman didn't even give you that.

I decided to lay it on the line.

"So what do you think Dr.? Can you help me?"

She looked up from her note pad as if I had disturbed her.

"I don't know Vincente. Were only scratching the surface. We have a lot of work to do. Why don't you tell me about your childhood?"

"Jesus Christ," I thought. "This is third grade Freud. Is this woman a fucking quack, or what?"

I thought about getting up and walking out, but I didn't. I figured I was already there so I might as well just go along with it. Make the best of a bad situation. I told her about my childhood. How I never really fit in. About how my teachers always thought I was bright, but yet a trouble maker at the same time. I told her about the bullies. The girls I had crushes on. The time I hadn't made the soccer team, and the inadequacy I felt. I told her everything. I went over on my time.

"I'm sorry Vincente, I think we are making a lot of headway, but were going to have to wrap this up. My next appointment will be here any minute." she said.

The goddamn greedy bitch! I wanted jump off the couch and strangle her.

"So now what do you think, Dr.? Do you have any advice?" I pleaded, still trying to maintain my composure.

A line of perspiration had formed across my lip.

"Maybe you should bring Rainy to a session with you." She said.

What! Was this woman insane! I didn't want to expose my soft under-belly to Rainy's ridicule. Plus, how could Rainy ever love or respect me if she knew what an emotional wreck I was.

"I don't think so, doc. I'm not sure that would be such a great idea."

"Why not?" She asked.

Obviously this woman hadn't learned a thing about me or my insecurities. I pulled a century-note from my wallet, handed it to her, thanked her for her time and said goodbye. I never went back.

When I got to Rainy's I noticed her mother's car in the parking lot. I ran my fingers through my hair and gave a sigh of exasperation. Now what?

I decided to keep circling the block until she was gone. The doctor had already wore me out. I didn't need Linda's shit too.

Chapter 37
(mid September)

It was fall once again and with the arrival of autumn I finally caught a break and found a job. I started working at one of those corporate home improvement centers, that put all the little mom and pop hardware stores under back in the 80's –Home Station: *Where your home is our home!* Or so the slogan went. But to tell you the truth, it wasn't any better than McKipson's.

I was brought in at minimum pay regardless of my previous customer-service experience, and was told that after three months I would be eligible for mediocre benefits (which would be sold to me at a premium price). After that the lady in H.R. gave me a number and a name badge, and told me to report to the Home Station, on the corner of fooled and robbed, at 5a.m. Saturday morning for orientation.

I went home feeling like a tremendous block of shit had been lifted off my shoulders. Like I could relax for a while. There is nothing worse than looking for a job. Needing a job. The person interviewing you always knows they have the upper hand. They know they have you just where they want you. And they use that opportunity to make you squirm.

"So why did you quit your last job?"

"What did you like least about your last job?"

"What did you like most?"

"Do you work well with others?"

"What are your weaknesses?"

"If hired how long do you plan to be with the company?"

"How many times in the last year were you tardy?"

"Red M&M's or blue?"

"Do you enjoy pornography?"

"Quickly, the square root of 576?"

It's jumping through hoops. And if you're not fast enough, or unable to fall with grace at the very least, there's a stack of applicants just waiting for your folly. You're only one fuck-up from being jobless. The machine eats cogs and spits them out like seeds. There's a million zombies out there that can do your job, and half of them probably better.

I showed up bright and early Saturday morning, with bells on as they say, I wanted to make a good impression, start off on the right foot. I was tired of having a boss on my ass. I decided I was going to do things right this time. I was going to become a lackey, a boot licker, an ass kisser. I had seen people do it all my life. Every place I ever worked had at least one teacher's pet. Someone who opted to kiss a little ass in lieu of working. I decided to join the path of least resistance and sell-out and come-up. I wasn't cut out to be a class warrior. I decided to let someone else fight the good fight for a while. At least until I crawled my way up to middle management, then I could take it back for the working-man. Yeah, I'd be like a secret agent or something. Taking down the infrastructure from the inside. Like that guy in the Ferlinghetti novel. The end would justify the means. I lied and told the lady from human resources I was looking to start a career and Home Station seemed the right place to do it. She ate it up. Happy as a pig in shit. I smiled to myself. James Bond couldn't have done it better.

There was at least fifty new employees at orientation, all as wide eyed and stupefied as me. We stood in the foyer uncertain of where to go. We looked like lost sheep yearning for a Sheppard. Christians about to be fed to the lions. Every Home Station employee that saw you, knew you were lost, knew you were new, but they zipped by leaving you to your stupor; not showing their hand. It was the same everywhere you went. Everyone was trying to hold on to the little edge they had over the next guy. Everyone was trying to postpone their imminent doom. I finally decided to just pick one of the other sheep and follow them till they found out where we were supposed to be. It was grammar school all over again −follow the kid in front of you. I picked a sheep with a nice plump ass and a tight pair of blue jeans. I followed her up plumbing, down electrical, through lumber, and over lighting, her tight ass wiggling all the way. It wasn't a bad way to start the day. I felt like a lion on the Serengeti, king of the jungle, stalking his weary pray. Each step bringing me closer to the moment I would pounce on her unexpecting ass.

After a couple of laps around the store blue-jeans finally found our way. We were to meet in this small room in the back of the store. Orientation would be held there. I expected to walk in and find an ornate table lined with assorted pastries and hot brewed coffee. The lady at human resources told me they liked to think, we at Home Station were a team, nay, a family! A place where one and all could feel at home!

Bullshit!

The room they were holding us up in looked like a make shift rat's nest. It wouldn't have sufficed as custodian's closet. The faux wood finishing on the tables was peeling, the chair's legs were all uneven, and the floor was an untiled concrete slab. Not so much as a box of Twinkies was in sight, and the coffee was nonexistent. Save for the VCR and big screen TV, the room resembled a third world classroom. Some family!

I walked in and found a seat up front. The star pupil. Spook in the making. People walked around, chit-chatted, and tried picking-up. I stared at the ceiling wondering what the hell I had gotten myself into this time.

Finally, the instructor walked in and the room fell to a silence. The women in awe. He was a massive brut. A man among men. Cut and toned. A god carved from granite. Fists like pig iron. The air of a drill instructor or gym coach wafted in behind him. I looked around at the women, then at Zeus, then my gut. I tried sucking it in.

"Welcome to Home Station," Zeus bellowed. "Where your not thought of as employees, but members!"

I felt a jerk inside my soul. A tiny eruption.

"I'm sorry, did you say members, or NUMBERS?"

Jesus Christ, where had that come from?! It just blurted out. An involuntary reaction. I looked around the room. No one was laughing. It was like a bad dream. People looked at me I like was something they had just stepped in. Blue-jeans nodded her head side to side in disapproval. I slouched down in my chair and tried to melt into my surroundings. I wanted to die and disappear. Zeus shot me a look like he was going to strangle me, then he composed himself.

"HA, HA, HA. No. Members. Where'dja get numbers? I guess it is early."

HA, HA, HA, the sheep laughed with Zeus. My dreams of being a freedom fighting spy had just slipped through my fingers, like shit through a sieve. My cover was blown. Damn, my fiery peasant's blood! I guess, in my heart of heart's, I was a revolutionary to the end. My grandfather's father had rode with Pancho Villa. That blood flowed through me. My revolutionary roots ran deep. You can't suppress something like that. It's undeniable.

After Zeus finished his little welcoming speech, which I had so rudely interrupted, he flipped off the lights and fired up the VCR. He showed us a video on proper lifting techniques, one on how NOT to sexually harass each other, another on hygiene and dress code, and he saved the best for last. It was a video starring the CEO's of Home Station, Jeff and Bob. They came to life through the electric glow of the television set. Two soft old men hiding behind fake yellow smiles; never worked a day in their life.

They stood in front of one of the stores in Spokane, WA. patting each other on the back. Two college kids on a field trip, congratulating each other for being masters of industry (it reminded me of Tommy McKipson). I could feel my stomach turn.

Why lord? Why them? What separated them from me?

It didn't make any sense. Some were destined to work, while for others, life was a carnival ride. I despised Jeff and Bob. They were evil personified. Cheesing it up for the camera like they were a couple of ordinary joe's. Pretending they hadn't made their fortune off the backs of a million nameless saps like me. Acting like they didn't have a house in the Hampton's while their children (who would eventually take hold of the plantation, and uphold the status quo, once their father's golf-course-tanned ass was rotting six feet under) attended ivy league schools. Who were these vampires set free to prey on the blood of the poor? And more over, where was my slice of the pie, Lord? Could you tell me that! Where was my slice of the pie?

Yes, I was sick. Sick with envy. I wanted their cars, women, and money. Why shouldn't I own a company? Hell, a small country! The meek and timid shall inherit the earth, phooey! I wanted my share and I wanted it now. I may have been born a peasant, but God mark my words, I wasn't going to die one! Why if I was king….

Snap!

I was brought back to reality by the flick of a light switch. Everyone was filing out of the room. Orientation was over. I walked out slowly, feeling alone and confused, not knowing where I belonged. I drove home under the hot Arizona sun. The light stinging my eyes. I was employed once again.

Chapter 38
(late September)

The only good thing about having a job was it got Rainy off my ass. Plus, it gave Linda one less thing to bitch about. And it enabled me to feel like a man again. So, maybe wage-slave was the best place for me.

Home Station hired me as a lot tech. Which is just a fancy way of saying I loaded up people's cars. I got to drive a forklift though, and that was pretty cool, until I smashed someone's tail-gate with the forks. The company had to pay for it. The boss didn't like that too much, but I didn't like the boss too much. As a matter of fact I didn't like him at all. He was this cross-eyed red neck from Texas. He was about 5 feet tall and had a little man's complex. He'd walk around all day bitching at us, chewing tobacco, and trying compensate for his stature. I wanted to kick his little hill-billy ass, but of course I never did.

Most of the girls seemed to like him though. Why, I don't know. He was a fucking cross-eyed, for Pete's sake. But women seem to have a thing for men in places of power, even if it is a home improvement center. Some day I'll be in charge, I thought to myself. Then it's my name they will scream. Yeah, right.

Most of the other managers were pretentious assholes as well, just like the ones I had worked for at the McKipson's –stooges vying for a colored vest and a gold name badge. At least there were lots of women. The women there automatically took a shining to me. I was fresh meat. And it helped that the other men that worked there were missing a couple of runs on the evolutionary ladder. Big apes with hairy forearms and enormous beer guts. Too bad for them, there was a new monkey in the jungle.

I started hanging out with a group of older female cashiers (late thirties) after work. There was a bar across the street and we would all go there for a few drinks. I loved it. Most of the time I wouldn't have to spend a dime. The girls would take turns buying me drinks. I just think they liked having a man along to keep the vultures off them. A lot of construction workers and contractors drank there, they liked to hit on the women, they never seemed to do it when I was there though. I know it had to piss them off to see this young guy getting all this attention from these older broads. I didn't care. Especially once I was drunk.

Me and the girls would stay there about three hours. They would sip their drinks and I'd put mine away, fast and furious. By the time I went home to Rainy I would be piss drunk. She didn't like that too much.

"Where the hell were you?"

"I told you I was going out for a drink after work."

"For three hours?"

"Yeah."

"This is fucking bullshit Vincente! At least three nights a week you go out with these whores! How many of them are you fucking?"

"Jesus Christ! I'm not fucking any of them! They're just friends!"

"Are you the only guy there."

"No! Dan and Mike were there too."

That was a bold face lie. I had to lie. I didn't want to, but Rainy would never fucking understand. I had to tell her what she wanted to hear. I was dependent on her for a place to stay. She would throw me out with the fucking trash if I didn't watch my ass. This shit was starting to get old. Every time I would go out for a drink I would have to listen to this shit when I got home. I started to feel like I was fucking married. Rainy always talked about my insecurities, but she was just as insecure. At least I could admit I feared being left alone, she couldn't even do that. For as strong as she tried to appear, she was really weak. Plus, she was pushing me away. Not that I think she knew it. I don't even think I knew it. We were too caught up. Too scared of being alone. Sometimes you have to remove yourself from a situation and stay away from it for a couple of months, before you can see what's really going on. People are weak. All of us are all weak. We get too caught up in our own lives and make more out of them then what they really are. It's an illusion. Me and Rainy should have called it quits right then. But we couldn't see it at the time. Too many emotions were involved, they were clouding our minds.

Chapter 39
(October)

Me and Rainy's relationship was slowly deteriorating, for good. And the longer I was at Home Station the worse it got. That's when I met

Debbie. One more chapter in my life. Another chance at love. I don't know what drew me to Debbie. By this time, I had pretty much came to the conclusion, women were strange creatures I would never understand. A smarter man would have called it quits, resorted to celibacy, the priest hood; hell, I don't know, I'm not a wise man. I think it was her innocence. That's what attracted me, her innocence.

Debbie worked in the garden department of Home Station, tending the plants. She was a 23 year old, bible-beating, virgin. She wasn't the looker that Rainy is (she didn't wear makeup or dress real flashy), but she had something. Maybe it was the whole, "opposites attract" thing. I mean, can you see me hanging around some abstinence-ring wearing chaste. Me and her couldn't have been bigger opposites. I started courting her, anyway though. While Rainy was at work I would take her out to dinner, ice cream shops, for long walks in the park. Sometimes we would just drive up to Mount Lemmon, and look at the city lights twinkling down below. We could park there, put the radio on, and just talk. It was nice. I felt relaxed around her. I didn't have to be drunk around her to feel comfortable, like I do with most women. Maybe it was because I knew sex wasn't an issue. She was saving it for marriage. When your worried about getting a piece of ass, it fogs your mind, you're on your guard constantly.

Debbie didn't like the fact that I went drinking with the immoral cashiers from up front, but she didn't hold it against me. I guess she thought she could break me of that bad habit. I think she saw me as a lost soul in need of guidance. A member of the flock who had strayed.

She wasn't a total prude though. Every time we'd go out she would let me feel her boobs over her shirt, and make-out with me, but trust me, that was the extent of it. Her legs were closed tighter than a church door, but I didn't mind. I started to develop serious feelings for Debbie. Thinking maybe we could settle down or something. I had never been with a virgin. Maybe that is what I needed, a woman who hadn't been defiled by another man's touch. We could buy a little place, have a couple kids, and go to church on Sundays. It didn't matter if I was an atheist or not. I was gonna reform myself, and become an upstanding citizen. Hell, maybe even a god fearing pillar of the community. Friend to man and beast alike. It was a nice dream. Then one day, you guessed it, everything came crashing down.

Chapter 40
(late October)

I came home one night, drunk again, after hanging out with the girls from work. Rainy was waiting for me on the front porch, smoking a cigarette, as I stumbled up.

"So, where were you tonight, you piece of shit? Fucking one of those whores from work?"

"Whatever, Rainy," I said making my way to the front door.

"Let me see your phone," she demanded standing to her feet.

Deep inside me something snapped. I had had enough. I was certifiably sick of Rainy's shit. I refused to put up with anymore of her crap. She had officially broke the camel's back. I had eaten a lot of shit over the last months, now it was her turn. I stood in front of her swaying slightly.

"Fuck you!" I said.

Her mouth fell open. She hadn't been expecting that one.

"I'm done letting you see my phone," I continued.

"What?" she said astounded.

"You heard me bitch, I ain't showing you my phone no more!"

Rainy rushed up trying to wrestle the phone out of my front pants pocket.

"What are you doing? Get the fuck off me bitch!" I said shrugging her off.

There is something I have noticed about unusually tall girls over the years –they are not very graceful. Rainy lost her footing and tripped over her own clumsy giraffe legs. She sat on the ground, on her big ass, with a skinned knee.

"YOU FUCKING ASSHOLE! YOU PUSHED ME! THAT'S ASSAULT! YOU FUCKING PUSHED ME! I'M CALLING THE COPS!"

"Go for it," I laughed. "You tripped yourself, you clumsy cunt."

"I FUCKING HATE YOU!" she screamed.

"I hate you too," I said stepping over her. "I don't even know why I'm with your ugly ass."

I could see her ego crumbling as the words left my mouth. It was a kill shot. The one thing that could destroy Rainy and her fragile self-image. She couldn't stand to think someone didn't find her beautiful. Especially me.

I stumbled inside, took my pants off, and crawled in to bed. I fell asleep clutching my phone to my chest.

I was awoken an hour later to blaring light and screaming.

"WAKE UP ASSHOLE! IT'S TIME FOR YOU TO GET THE FUCK OUT OF HERE!"

I was startled and disoriented. I was still drunk. I was trying to grasp what was going on, but I was out of it. My phone lay open next to me.

"WHO THE FUCK IS DEBBIE?"

How did she know about Debbie? Everything was whirling around me. I thought maybe I was dreaming. Actually I hoped I was. I started to get out of bed.

"I LISTENED TO YOUR MESSAGES, WHO THE FUCK IS DEBBIE?"

I figured Rainy was bluffing. I didn't remember receiving any messages that night. I made my way to the kitchen. I needed a glass a water.

"WHERE ARE YOU GOING? YOU NEED TO GET THE FUCK OUT OF HERE! GRAB YOUR SHIT AND GO!

I looked at the floor and Rainy had packed all my shit into a box. It wasn't much, mostly clothes and stuff. I said nothing and started to put on my pants, then made my way to the box. The jig was up. I figured I'd forgo the water.

"THAT'S RIGHT GET YOUR SHIT AND LEAVE!"

I grabbed the box, put on my shoes and made my way to the door, still drunk and disoriented, never saying a word. I had had enough. I didn't want to fight anymore. There was no point. I just wanted to leave. Rainy had won. I was a broke and defeated man.

As I walked out the front door and made my way to the parking lot, Rainy continued to follow me, mocking me all the way. Saying the most vile shit.

"YOU'RE FUCKING DISGUSTING VINCENTE! I HOPE YOU GET AIDS AND DIE YOU PIECE OF SHIT! HOW CAN YOU STAND YOURSELF...."

I said nothing and continued to make my way to my car. All of a sudden Rainy turned around and ran back to the condo, she reappeared a second later with her arms full of stuff. It was everything I had bought her during the course of our relationship: stuffed animals, pictures of us, bottles of perfume, dried bouquets of roses, etc. etc.. She looked at me and heaved it all into the dumpster, then ran back over to where I was pulling out and preparing to drive off.

"I FUCKING HATE YOU!" she screamed before spitting on my windshield.

The spit stuck to the glass and slid down slowly, obscuring my view. I turned the wipers on and gave the window a blast of water. All the filth wiped away. I drove off leaving Rainy and all the ugliness behind me.

When I got down the street I pulled out my phone and listened to my messages. There was only one. It was from Debbie.

"Hi, babe. I was calling to see what you were doing tonight. I thought maybe we could get together. Hope to hear from you, bye."

I must of missed her call while I was at the bar. I couldn't believe how careless I had been. I usually always checked and erased my messages to prevent something like this from happening. It was my own fault.

Oh well.

At least now I was free of Rainy. Maybe now I could build something meaningful with Debbie.

I had no other place to go, so I headed over to my cousin Mona's place. I knew she would always have a couch for me to crash on.

I woke up the next morning on Mona's couch, hung-over, but optimistic. I figured all of this happening was probably for the best. The longer me and Rainy were together the worse it would have got.

Mona made toast and coffee for the both of us, then I picked some clothes out of my box, took a shower, and got ready to go to work. David and Chad didn't seem too keen on having me show up at three in the morning to crash on the couch, but I didn't give a fuck. If they didn't like it, they could go blow each other.

As I drove to work I tried to stay optimistic. I kept telling myself everything was gonna work itself out. I was completely unprepared for the nuclear fallout I was about to face.

Chapter 41
(late October)

As I pulled into the Home Station parking lot I was greeted by Rainy's car. I could feel my stomach jump-up in to my throat. What the fuck was she doing here? I walked inside, prepared for the worst, and wasn't let down.

Rainy was standing in the front of the store berating Debbie as Rick (the cross-eyed, red-neck, manager) tried to quell the situation. Rainy was calling Debbie a whore and blaming her for wrecking our relationship. Debbie was trying to explain that she had no idea I was involved with someone (which she didn't), but Rainy wasn't buying it. I could see the terror in Debbie's eyes as Rainy's nearly six foot frame towered over her, she looked like she wanted to cry. I felt bad.

"Mam, you're creating a scene. I'm gonna hafta ask ya ta leave," Rick said, his words falling on deaf ears.

I walked up and accosted Rainy. A small crowd was starting to gather around.

"What the fuck are you doing here?" I asked. "This is my job, bitch!"

Rainy turned around and slapped me across the face –hard. Tiny flashes of light danced before my eyes. In unison the crowd that had gathered said, "Oooooooo!"

Rick looked at me. "Do you know this Gal, Vincente?" he asked.

Rainy continued to scream at Debbie. It looked like it might boil over into violence at any moment.

"She's my ex-girlfriend," I said.

"Well, get 'er outta here!" said Rick.

"What do you think I'm trying to do, you dwarf!"

Rick gave me a dirty look and returned his attention to Rainy.

"Look missy, if you don't leave right now, I have no other choice but to call the authorities!"

Rainy spun around facing Rick. Then she addressed the crowd that had gathered.

"I'M LEAVING. I JUST WANT EVERYONE HERE TO KNOW THAT VINCENTE VASQUEZ IS A CHEATING PIECE OF SHIT, AND THIS LITTLE SLUT HERE IS ONE OF HIS WHORES!"

Then she calmly turned around and walked out while straightening her hair. And as simple as that it was over.

After a couple of minutes, realizing that the action was over, the crowd slowly started to dissipate. Debbie looked at me, for the first time during this whole fiasco, and began to sob uncontrollably. Rick asked that I follow him to the office and tender my resignation. It was either that or be fired. I told him to just go ahead and fire me as I walked out, throwing my apron on the floor. Debbie never talked to me again, or returned my calls. It was simple as that. Rainy had won.

As I drove out of the parking lot I wondered what else life had in store for me. How low could one man sink? I had no choice now but to move in with my parents.

Chapter 42
(late October)

I felt like a complete loser living at my parent's house. I was almost twenty-four and going nowhere. And since my parents had long since turned my old bedroom into a storage room/office, I had no place to stay but the couch. I had hit rock bottom. I couldn't sink any lower.

Every morning I would have to listen to my father tell me how he thought I should go back to school and become an accountant. It had been his life-long dream to have an accountant for a son. Since my kid brother was going to school for physical therapy, I was his last hope to fulfill his dream. But I couldn't even fulfill my own dreams, how could I help him with his?

I spent all day sleeping, and all night watching infomercials for things like Wonder Chamois and food dehydrators. I wore the same pair of dirty shorts for days on end. Occasionally my cousin Mona, or Santos and Emma, would try to get a hold of me, but I would never return their calls. I was becoming a shut-in of Howard Hughes proportions. All the days began to blend together. I stopped eating and was perpetually anxious. I was losing my grip with reality and spiraling toward a nervous breakdown. My parents stared at me in awe, uncertain what to make of their eldest son. And then, before I knew it, it was Halloween.

Since I had nowhere to go, and no one to spend the evening with, I decided to dress up and hand candy out to all the kids. I figured the fresh night air would do me good. I went to the bathroom to apply my costume. Since I didn't have any face paint I figured I could just use my mom's makeup. I painted dark circles around my eyes with eye-liner, then used some red lipstick to paint some fake blood trickling from the corner of my mouth. To finish off my costume I got a small length of rope from my fathers shed and made a noose for my neck. I had decided to go as a suicide victim. I looked in the mirror and liked what I saw. I looked great. So I sat on the front porch with a big bowl of candy and let the kids come to me.

Sitting there by myself, I couldn't help but think about last year's Halloween. It was the first time me and Rainy had hooked up. For some reason, I don't know why, I started to cry.

A little boy walked and saw me. He must have been all of four. He was dressed like Spider-Man.

"What's wrong, mister? Why are you crying?" he asked.

"I think I'm dead," I said.

His mother rushed up and spirited him away from me with a terrified look on her face. I decided I better go back inside, before somebody called the cops or the nut-house.

Once inside I felt like the walls were closing in on me. Everything suddenly felt unfamiliar. The roof started to spin and I became dizzy. My heart pumped like mad. I laid on the couch ,closed my eyes and prayed for sleep. It was slow to come. And when it did it was restless.

Chapter 43
(November)

Miracle Mile was an ailing 1.5 mile strip of poorly paved road between I-10 and Oracle road, where anything could be had: prostitutes, pornography, drugs, violence, you name it. And despite it's name, I had yet to hear of any "miracles" taking place there. Well, except for maybe one.

In the 30's it had been the northwest gateway into Tucson and home to a thriving hotel and hospitality industry. Weary travelers, hungry for auto-centered tourist culture, would flock to Miracle Mile's state-of-the-art motor-courts, flashing neon signs, and it's crown jewel: The Ghost Ranch Lodge (a lavish desert oasis situated on eight acres of scenic desert landscape, with winding pathways, sunning patios and vast lawn areas). Designed by renowned Tucson architect Josias Joesler, The Ghost Ranch Lodge (and its iconic cow-skull logo created by the famous flower artist, Georgia O'Keeffe), had been a Tucson favorite for over three decades. That's until the 1960's brought the completion of I-10 (diverting travelers away from Miracle Mile and hurting business), and the convenience of inexpensive airline travel effectively ended the era of leisurely auto treks. After that, the strip began a slow decline and by the 80's it was one of the worst shit holes in Tucson. A cesspool of violence and decay.

After a month of sitting on my parent's couch like a depressed suicidal bum, I figured it was time I get out and engage in some good ol' fashioned, destructive behavior. It was either that or off myself, and I wasn't quite ready for that. Things weren't all that bad yet, and since Halloween I had made a slight emergence from my deep depression, however, I was still far from being out of the woods.

I hadn't had a drink since Rainy gave me the boot, and I was itching like mad for one.

I knew of this seedy strip club on Miracle Mile, so I made that my destination. I figured, why not see some titties while I drink. Plus, I hadn't had the companionship of a woman in some time. And, like Holden Caulfield before me, sometimes I thought it was just nice to be around girls. To smell them. Talk to them. Hear their voice. Even if I was paying for their company.

So there I was, sitting in the back of the club, wallowing in existential ennui, wondering how I had come to this point. Wondering how I had sunk so low? I had made a complete wreck of my life. I had no job, no home, no woman –nothing. I was my own worst enemy. I sat there, drunk, sipping my beer and thinking. The speakers overhead rattled, the bass being emitted, threatening to tear them apart.

Just then, a beautiful black girl took the stage –a cat, sensuous and sleek. She moved like a smooth jazz sample, her ample hips swinging back and forth to the dreary beat, a virtual slave to the rhythm. She was the most beautiful thing I had ever seen. She must have saw me staring at her, because as soon as the song ended she sauntered off stage and made her way to me.

"Would you like a dance?" she asked.

"Sure," I said.

She didn't waste any time and went straight to work on me, grinding, grabbing my cock. She brushed her nipples across my lips and let me put my hands on her hips. She was good. Real good. She had thick pouty lips, a firm round ass, and a sweet musky scent. I could see the bouncer eyeing me from the corner of the room so I kept the touching to a minimum.

Touching was a big no-no in strip clubs. The girls could touch you all they wanted (if they chose to) but it was forbidden for patrons to do any touching of their own. Technically it was illegal for the girls to touch the patrons as well, (the state viewed it as prostitution), but since the girls were the ones who tipped the bouncers out (and touching horny guys is how you made big bucks), the bouncers usually turned a blind-eye to it. That being said, occasionally, the bouncers would let patrons cop a feel as well (as long as the girls were cool with it), that way the money kept flowing in all directions, and one hand washed the other one.

The longer she danced for me, the more aroused I became. My libido, which had been lying dormant for the last month, was now back with a vengeance. My dick got so hard I thought it would split my pants. Something over came me, maybe it was the booze, but at this moment, I was certain this girl wanted me as much as I wanted her. My mind was racing. I didn't know what to do. Fuck it, I thought.

I grabbed the back of her head and thrusted it towards mine, trying to slip my tongue between her lips. She pushed herself off of me and slapped me across the face –hard. "Motherfucker!", she said looking at me in disbelief. The bouncer rushed over and grabbed me by the shirt. He was big, real big, at least three inches taller than me.

"Come on asshole," he grunted. "time to go!"

"Get your paws off me you fucking ape!' I shouted coming to my feet.

The alcohol was playing on my mind. Giving me strength I didn't possess. "I could take this guy," I found myself thinking. "Despite his 22 inch biceps and his 44 inch chest, I could fuck him up."

"So, do you wanna do this the easy or the hard way?" the man-mountain asked.

This was it. I was gonna fuck this guy up. I was gonna release the last three year's frustrations, on this goon, in one colossal ass whoppin'. He had screwed with the wrong guy. I was a caged animal. A fuckin' monster! He just didn't know.

"Let me take a piss," I said. "then we'll do this the hard way."

The giant's face turned to stone. The anger left his eyes and was replaced with bewilderment. He didn't know what to think. Was I fucking crazy?

I walked to the bathroom calm and confident, a regular Dirty Harry.

As I stood there pissing I imagined my foe vanquished, the stun look on the dancer's faces, the respect and admiration of my fellow patrons. Vincent the giant killer, they'd call me. Slayer of dragons. I walked out of the bathroom ready for war. I didn't make it three feet. It was an ambush.

Quinbus Flestrin had one of his brethren sneak up behind me, and secure me in a three-quarter nelson, as he walked over and sucker punched me in the gut. My diaphragm quivered as the air escaped my mouth and lungs. I gasped like a fish on land and flailed feebly in an attempt to free myself. The giant leaned over and hissed in my ear, "You said you wanted it the hard way," then he proceeded to punch me in the face. Flashes of light appeared before my eyes. Twinkling stars. The big dipper. Ursa major. Orion.

The next thing I knew I was laying, face down on the pavement, outside. Polyphemus stood over me taunting.

"Don't come back or you'll get more of the same asshole!"

"Yeah," his buddy said in agreeance before they slammed the door.

I picked myself up and decided to walk home. I was too drunk to drive. And besides, I couldn't find my keys. I figured the bouncers had stolen them in the scuffle and chucked them somewhere.

As I walked down the street, once a shining beacon to highway commerce, I was taken with a brilliant idea –I would call Roo! I had a sudden, unexplainable urge to talk to her. As a matter of fact, I had never wanted to do anything more. Maybe she would invite me over, I thought. Hell, maybe we would even reconcile.

I dialed the number from memory. It rang and rang. No one answered. I decided I better try again. Maybe I had dialed the wrong number. It was more of the same though, endless ringing.

What now?

More brilliant ideas.

I decided to call Trish, my old fall back, I hadn't talked to her since that night she called me crying. I wanted to apologize for my behavior and tell her I was sorry for the way I had treated her. Plus, I thought I might be able to hook up with her for old time's sake.

As I walked down the street with my phone in my hand, trying to remember Trish's number, some one called out to me.

"Yo, man!"

It was some black dude (now this wasn't that friendly brother from the insurance office that helps you with your policy, or your sophomore calculus professor, this was Dookie from the hood, a grimy looking brother) sitting on the stoop of one of the old dilapidated hotels (a lot of them now doubled as cheap one bedroom apartments). I figure he either wanted to sell me drugs, roll me, or turn me on to some hoes. Either way, I wasn't interested in any of it. I kept on walking.

"Hey, man!" he called after me.

I got about another 10 feet down the road when someone rolled up next to me on a bike. It was that fool from the stoop. His bike looked about two sizes too small for him. I wondered where he had stole it from.

"Yo, let me use your phone," he said.

I looked him up and down. He had a doo-rag on, a scar across his face, and a gold tooth. Did he think I was stupid? I knew what neighborhood I was in. Plus this dude looked like a fucking crook. I would never see my phone again.

"Nah, man, you can't use my phone," I said.

"Come on, man."

"Nah."

"Don't be a little bitch!"

"Fuck you! How did you get that scar, sucking dick?"

That pissed him off. He looked like he wanted to punch me. But I towered over him and weighed 260 lbs. I didn't look like an easy fight. Plus, anybody walking alone in this neighborhood at night had to be packin' heat, or fucking crazy. He decided it wasn't worth it. Not while he was alone.

"Yo, me and my homeboys are gonna fuck you up! They're right around the corner. You fucked up now, son!"

I watched him speed off and turn the corner next to the Tropicana, adult video theater. I figured he was bluffing. Till I saw a couple of guys come out of the shadows. There was five of them total and they looked pissed. I had done it now.

I wasn't prepared to get my ass whooped, I had to think quick. I ran across the street to Evergreen cemetery. I figured I could cut through there and come out the other side on Oracle road, safe and secure.

When I got across the street There was a little brick wall surrounding that side of the cemetery. It was only about three feet tall. I figured I could hop over it easily. So that's what I did. Once on the other side though, I started to fall. I tumbled through the darkness for what seemed like an eternity, feet over head and head over feet. No one told me a ditch lay on the other side!

I finally hit the bottom, feet first. The rest of my body wasn't far behind. I was face down in the dirt, scraped and bruised.

I jumped up and started to run again. A sharp pain emitted from my ankle. I had twisted it when I hit the ground. I was no longer running but limping. I could hear people behind me, I couldn't stop. I ran till I thought my heart would explode (which wasn't very far, I was in terrible shape). When I couldn't go on any further, I ducked down behind a large tombstone, and panted like crazy. My lungs felt like they were on fire. My throat felt like it had been rubbed raw with sandpaper. I sat there listening, breathing heavily and trying to be quiet. I couldn't hear anything, I figured I had lost them, but I wasn't taking any chances, I decided to wait awhile longer. As I sat there my eyelids grew heavy. It was pitch black and silent save for the beating of my heart. A darkness washed over me and with it sleep. And as I slept I dreamt.

I dreamed I was standing on the horizon of a vast open plain. It stretched as far as the eyes could see and was covered with numerous small ponds, large weeping willows, and short manicured grass of a brilliant green. I walked between the ponds, and around the willows, until one of the ponds seemed to call my name. I stopped curiously to gaze into it. It was crystal clear and seemed to be immeasurably deep, there was no bottom, only a black void hinting at the infinite vastness. As I sat staring at my own reflection a large gray, armor plated, prehistoric looking, fish came out of the darkness. It had to be about the size of a Volkswagen Beetle. It had spiked fins and enormous, ominous, white eyes situated on the front of it's fishy face. The cold soulless eyes were absent of pupils and possessed only a iridescent pearl like sheen. One look at it's eyes and it was obvious this creature was an inhabitant of the pond's deep, murky blackness.

It moved slowly and purposefully towards the pond's surface. Its small, swaying, caudal fin moving it's immense body. When it reached the surface we stood staring at each other. This denizen of the deep's eerie eyes, seemed to pierce my soul. And just when I thought I couldn't bear it's gaze a second longer, it languidly opened its toothy, frog like, mouth. What I saw made my flesh creep.

Inside the fish's mouth was a small boy of about 5 or 6. He was pale and lifeless. His sandy brown hair danced in the calm water. His fingers were cold and gray. Then his head slowly rolled to the side and I could see his white lifeless eyes, they looked just like the fish's. It made chills run down my spine, but the most disturbing part was –the boy was me.

Terrified by the image I turned and ran from that place. But the faster I tried to escape the slower my progress. The green grass became quicksand beneath my feet, pulling me under, into the abyss. I grasped at the air, but to no avail. The earth slowly swallowed me. It was too late. The darkness was complete.

Chapter 44
(November)

I awoke the next morning to a rake handle poking me in the ribs. An elderly grounds keeper was standing over me.

"Are joo okay?" he asked me.

I looked around me confused. Where was I? The sun was barely peeking over the mountains in the horizon. It was that magic hour between night and day. I started to realize, I must have passed out some time during the night and used a tombstone for my pillow.

"*Si tata*, I was just taking a nap," I assured him.

"If joo say, so," he said skeptically as he walked away.

My brain felt like a dried up sponge lying in my skull. There wasn't any way I could hold my head where it didn't hurt. It throbbed with pain. I stood up, ready to get the hell out of there, forgetting that I had twisted my ankle the night before. The pain almost dropped me to my knees. I lifted my pant leg. It looked like I was trying to smuggle a grapefruit in my sock. I held on, to one of the nearby tombstones for support, and cursed myself. Could it get any worse?

My life seemed like one big joke played against me. I stumbled at every turn. Had God cursed me? What was I doing wrong? Was this all my fault? Would I ever win?

As I hobbled my way out of the cemetery I saw an old lady placing some fresh flowers on somebody's grave. Maybe her husband's. Maybe her son's. At least I'm still alive I thought. Maybe things weren't as bad as they seemed. I had escaped *Cool and the Gang* last night, that was a positive.

And at least I had my parents couch to sleep on. There were people out there that didn't even have that. Hell, Miracle Mile was living proof of that. As I made my way to Oracle road, all of a sudden, I had an epiphany.

Maybe my life wasn't so bad after all. I mean, it could always be worse, right? At least I was still breathing. As long as that was going on, I had a fighting chance. Perhaps, all I needed was a change of venue, a new town. Maybe, If I could just start over some place new, everything would start looking up. I headed east, in the direction of the sun, my objective was clear as day. All I needed to do was get out of Tucson, and it's damn dry heat.

ABOUT THE AUTHOR

Steven Eggleton was born in Tucson, Arizona in 1976. He started writing poetry and prose in 2001 and published his first short-story in 2004. He is a two time college dropout and holds the distinction of being a completely self-taught writer. Eggleton is married and is the father of two beautiful young girls. He continues to live and work in Tucson, his favorite city.